W9-CCJ-631

Also by André Brink

An Act of Terror
A Chain of Voices
Looking on Darkness
The Ambassador
States of Emergency
Mapmakers
A Land Apart (with J. M. Coetzee)
The Wall of the Plague
An Instant in the Wind
Rumours of Rain
A Dry White Season

A Story

André Brink

Simon & Schuster

The First Life of Adamastor

New York London Toronto Sydney Tokyo Singapore

SIMON & SCHUSTER
Simon & Schuster Building
Rockefeller Center
1230 Avenue of the Americas
New York, New York 10020

Designed by Hyun Joo Kim
Illustrations by Julie Metz
Manufactured in the United States of America

1 3 5 7 9 10 8 6 4 2

Library of Congress Cataloging-in-Publication Data

Brink, André Philippus, date.
Cape of storms : the first life of Adamastor : a story / by André Brink.
p. cm.
1. Adamastor (Legendary character)—Fiction. I. Title.
PR9369.3.B7C36 1993
823—dc20 92-39321
CIP

ISBN 0-671-79907-X

Quotations in Chapter 1 from Canto V of the *Lusiads* are from the translation by J. J. Aubertin (Kegan Paul, London, 1884).

This is the use of memory:
For liberation—not less of love but expanding
Of love beyond desire, and so liberation
From the future as well as the past.

—T. S. Eliot

Introduction

In which, after some critical remarks about early French and Portuguese interpretations of Adamastor, the narrator proposes the terms of his contract with the reader

Once upon a time there was and there wasn't. A formula I found in a book I can no longer trace, on the history of narrative forms. An old Spanish tradition, I believe, and particularly useful in the present context, where distinctions between *was* and *wasn't* are rather blurred. Rabelais, to my knowledge the first to introduce

Adamastor* in a story, does not shed much light on the subject. His character rates a mere mention (*Pantagruel,* Chapter 1) in the long genealogy of giants who begat one another, among them the hundred-handed Briareus, culminating of course in Gargantua and Pantagruel ("... Briare, qui avoit cent mains, Qui engendra Prophyric, Qui engendra Adamastor, Qui engendra Antee ...").

Camões, who may well have been familiar with Rabelais before embarking on his own *Lusiads* (1572), places the giant among the Titans who rebelled against Zeus ("Qual Egeo e o Centimano"—the latter once again a creature with a hundred hands). Admittedly, in his version, in the justly famous Canto V, Adamastor is not a giant to be treated without respect. When Vasco da Gama and his crew on their precarious voyage around Africa to the spicy and miraculous East are confronted by this "horrid monster," he addresses them in lofty rhetoric:

> "I am that mighty Cape occult and grand
> Who by you all 'The Stormy' named has been"—

which resounds even more splendidly in the original:

> "Eu sou aquelle occulto e grande Cabo,
> A quem chamais vós outros Tormentorio."

---

* *In Greek,* adamastos *signifies "wild," "untamed."*

But in the final analysis the Adamastor conceived by Camões is more revolting than impressive, "Of stature all deformed and vast and tall,/The visage frowning, and with squalid beard;/The eyes were hollow, and the gesture all/Threatening and bad; the colour pale and seared;/And full of earth and grizzly was the hair;/The mouth was black, the teeth all yellow were."

His tragedy, as explained by Camões, lies in his consuming love for Thetis,* Nymph and Princess of the Wave, whom he has seen but once, fleetingly and fatally, as she was bathing naked with her Nereids on the shore:

> ". . . no power my sense could save,
> I felt by love o'ercome in such a way
> That nought I know I'd long for more to-day."

It is inconceivable that his love can ever be requited. "What love of nymph could e'er suffice/To cope with that of giant of this size?" asks our pretentious poet. But here I must protest. My own suspicion, the product no doubt of a more cynical and secular age, is that if the lack of response to the poor creature's amorous advances had indeed been partly caused by a discrepancy in size, this may well have involved only one part of his anatomy. On this, perhaps with the best of intentions, Camões seizes, taking *pars pro toto,* blowing up, in a manner of speaking, out of all proportion a stum-

---

* *Her spouse was Peleus, and she was later the mother of Achilles.*

bling block that might well have been overcome with some patience and considerable pleasure. As if that were not enough, he drags the nymph's mother Doris into a particularly dirty plot to trick the giant.

In exchange for a promise that Adamastor will cease his war against the armies of the Sea, she undertakes to arrange a nocturnal tryst with her oh-so-innocent daughter:

> "Already fooled, already war denied,
> At last one night, by Doris promised, shone,
> When from afar the beauteous form I spied
> of Thetis white, unrobed, and all alone."

But when, "mad-like," he approaches to take the fair maid in his arms and proceeds to attempt what hopefully seems natural to both,

> "I found within my arms a rugged mount,
> With harshest wood and thorny thickets faced;
> Standing before a rock, e'en front to front,
> Clasped for her own angelic form in haste,
> I was not a man, but deaf and dumb by shock,
> And fixed against one rock another rock!"

This disillusionment coincides with Zeus's decision finally to punish the rebellious Titans. Some of them, as we know from Greek mythology, are buried under huge mountains;

Adamastor is turned into the jagged outcrop of the Cape Peninsula:

> "Into hard earth my flesh converted lies,
> My bones are turned to rocks all rough and
> strange,
> These members and this form ye see, likewise,
> Extended through these spreading waters range;
> In fine, my stature of enormous size
> Into this Cape remote the Gods did change;
> While for redoubled anguish of my woes,
> Thetis around me in these waters flows."

Rather exaggerated; but that is what happens to the truth when writers get their hands on it. And all of this is offered as a mere background to the somber prophecy Camões makes Adamastor utter (bearing in mind that what had been prophecy for da Gama and his crew had already become history for the contemporaries of Camões): shipwrecks, and all manner of catastrophes awaiting the explorers of the Cape of Storms, a litany of destruction, despair and death:

> "And here I hope to take, if not misled,
> 'Gainst him deep vengeance who discovered
> me."

His apocalyptic prophecies culminate in a vision worthy of that age of overstatement:

"Another too shall come of honoured fame,
Liberal and generous and with heart enchained,
And with him he shall bring a lovely dame,
Whom through Love's favouring grace he shall
   have gained;
Sad fate, dark fortune nought can e'er reclaim,
Call them to this my realm, where rage unreined
Shall leave them after cruel wreck alive,
With labours insupportable to strive.

"Their children shall die starving in their sight,
Who were in such affection bred and born;
They shall behold by Caffres' grasping might
Her clothing from the lovely lady torn;
Shall see her form, so beautiful and white,
To heat, cold, wind, expos'd, and all forlorn,
When she has trod o'er leagues and leagues of
   land
With tender feet upon the burning sand.

"And more those eyes shall witness, which sur-
   vive,
Of so much evil and so much mischance:
Shall see the two sad lovers, just alive,
Into the dense unpitying woods advance;
There, where the hearts of very stones they rive
With tears of grief and anguished sufferance,
In fond embrace their souls they shall set free
From the fair prison of such misery."

In many ways this is an unsatisfactory translation; yet something of the great original melodrama shines through it, as baroque and exaggerated as the arches and architraves, the sheer excess, the inspired bad taste of the Manueline churches and cloisters in Lisbon or Oporto.

Bearing all of this in mind—and reacting to the suggestion of eurocentric revulsion implicit in that image of the mighty cape, occult and grand, with its deformed stature, frowning visage, squalid beard, black mouth and yellow teeth—I have been nagged for a long time now by a particular question: from what "raw material" could Camões have fashioned his typically sixteenth-century European version of the story? Is it possible that behind it looms an original, an unwritten Urtext? And if so, could this conceivably be reconstructed in our own time and terms?

This is the motivation behind my present venture. More precisely, my hypothesis is this: suppose there *were* an Adamastor, a model for the giant of Camões's fanciful history; and suppose that original creature, spirit, or whatever he may have been, has survived through the centuries in a series of disparate successive avatars in order to continue watching over the Cape of Storms: how would *he* look back, from the perspective of the late twentieth century, on that original experience?

This is the leap I propose to take; and my reader is invited to take the plunge with me.

1

In which the reader encounters a curious kind of bird, and a woman hatched from an egg

Now that really was a sight to behold. From the sea, from the nesting place of the sun, we could see two objects swimming toward us, looking for all the world like two enormous seabirds with white feathers fluttering in a breeze that had newly sprung up. Not far from the beach, where our people were gathering mussels from the rocks exposed by the ebb tide, the two birds came to rest and appeared to draw in their feathers. Made no attempt to come closer to the shore. Just stayed there, bobbing on the swell, waiting perhaps for fish, but in that case it must have been whales, they were so huge. After a long time our eyes prised a third seabird loose from the horizon, all the way from where sea and sky lay together in the blue to where it joined the first two. And then, much later, yet another. Then a strange thing happened. While we were still standing there staring, the two birds in front began to lay eggs of a curious roundish shape, and brown in color. (What the two at the back were doing we couldn't make out; for all we knew they were males.) What amazed us was that these eggs did not emerge, as one would expect, from the tail end of the birds, but rather from under their wings; and soon the eggs came drifting toward us on the tide. They had hardly reached the shore when people started hatching from them,* not one at a time, but whole bunches.

Well, people. We'd seen all kinds of human beings before. People like us, the *Khoikhoin* who'd inhabited these parts ever since the rock time of *Tsui-Goab*; and *San* (whom later generations of white foreigners would call "Bushmen"); and high up near the Upper River the Angry People we called the Xhosa had lived for longer than anyone could remember. But people like the ones that were hatched from those eggs we'd never ever set eyes on before. Like birds you might say, all colors under the sun; we first thought it was feathers but then we made out it was a kind of clothing. And strutting about stiff-legged like ostriches, and their heads so overgrown with beards and mustaches you could hardly see

---

* *About four centuries later, in 1897, the early Afrikaans poet S. J. du Toit used a similar image in his poem "Hoe die Hollanders die Kaap Ingeneem Het" ("How the Dutch Conquered the Cape"), probably borrowed from stories circulating freely at the Cape. But he talks about geese giving birth to little ones from their sides, which is patently ridiculous. Birds lay eggs. Including those we saw. I know; I was there.*

their faces. Just as well, for they didn't seem to have much in the line of skin, all pale and white like grass that had grown under a rock for too long.

I cannot say for sure today that they were Vasco da Gama and his men on their way to or from the East (on their first journey, or another?); or perhaps their predecessors, Bartholomeu Dias and his crew, who'd rounded our Cape a decade earlier (1488); or others following in their wake. Now I have of course seen copies of paintings and tapestries of da Gama, and that square man in his drapes and embroidery, the puffed striped sleeves, the beard and mustache, sporting on his chest the Cross of Aviz, does look familiar; but can one trust a painting, especially one made so long after the event? Moreover, all those people looked alike to us; if you'd seen one you'd seen them all. Except for the woman, of course. *She* was different! But even that might have escaped me had I not chanced upon her* unencumbered by the wad of clothing they'd all wrapped themselves in. Naked, smooth, white, and all alone. Oh yes, she was different, all right; the most different thing I had ever seen. As unbelievable as if she'd just that moment risen from the white seed of our father Heitsi-Eibib, inimitable hunter. Like a thin tongue of fire, a bitter spark released that instant from a flintstone struck by none other than Tsui-Goab. In the course of my lives I have seen, and had, and been had by, innumerable women; but that first sight of the one I later named *Khois* (which means, of course,

---

* *See the following chapter.*

Woman), is beyond comparison with anything else. My only innocence, perhaps. So bear with me.

On that first afternoon there was no sight or trace of her. To tell the truth, those eggs had barely touched the coast and hatched their motley brood when all of us scampered off the rocks, across the stretch of beach, over the first row of dunes, and into the dense bush beyond. The sun was already squatting over its nest before we came to a standstill. And it was a cold and hungry night for us as we'd abandoned all our food and implements among the rocks. All night long we huddled beside our fire listening to the hyenas whooping and the jackals laughing in the dark; not even the deep grunts of a marauding lion could scare us. Not after we'd seen what no human eyes had seen before; and it was only when Tsui-Goab, the Red Dawn, returned, smudging the sky with the blood of his latest kill, that we began to feel secure enough to approach the thing with words. It was I they all turned to for advice. I was their leader. In that life my name was T'kama, which means Big Bird. In normal parlance this meant Ostrich, but in the Khoi language "bird" is also a slang word for the male member; so I humbly trust, as I am not given to self-advertisement, that the reader will draw his (or indeed her) own conclusions.

And so I was known as T'kama, the son of T'kaneep, the man with the bird that never came to rest.

And he the son of Gubu, whom they called The Man with a Hundred Hands because man alone he could wage war against more enemies than anyone could count.

And he the son of Aob, who killed the lion.

The son of Ghaihantimu, who could play the *gurah* like no one else.

The son of Goro, who first crossed the Great River and brought back stories nobody had heard before.

The son of Akambi, who had killed his twin brother inside the womb of their mother and was born with only one ball.

The son of K'guda, the Gazelle, who could run faster than the West Wind.

The son of the Great Magician.

The son of the one whose mother had been a wildebeest.

And so back, back, back, all the way to the time of Heitsi-Eibib and beyond, to where Tsui-Goab had first fashioned the solid rock bed of the earth and then had broken stones from it and blown breath into them and turned them into human beings. Kanima, the first man, the Ostrich Feather; and his wife, Haunamaos, the Yellow Copper.

I gave the people my advice. We first went back to the huts we'd set up a mere full moon ago in the opening among the fat-fingered trees today's people call euphorbias, and which we'd completely bypassed in our stampede the night before to prevent the Beard Men from following us and discovering our place. The predators abroad in the night had caused all our fat-tailed sheep to break from their kraal and it took us all day to round them up again and repair the hedge of white-thorn branches. From sunset, and throughout the night, we sang and made music and danced and prayed to Tsui-Goab; and at dawn we pissed on the dying coals of the fire, and sprinkled fresh water from pots and calabashes at the entrance to the huts. Only then did we return to the beach.

From the coarse scrub on the dunes we watched the eggs returning to the land (during the night the birds must have kept them under their wings) and the men setting to work on the beach. They fetched water from the shallow stream running into the bay just beyond the first ridge of rocks. They washed their clothes. A group of them disappeared into the bush, to look for food most likely. Some time afterward there was a strange thunderclap in the distance, which we could not explain as there wasn't a cloud in the whole pale expanse of the sky; and after another while they returned with a dead springbok, carried by two of them, suspended from a pole on their shoulders. The sort of thing we had been doing all our lives. So they seemed like ordinary human beings after all.

What we found especially reassuring was this: when the sun was right overhead a new group of men came to the shore in an egg from one of the seabirds and dragged an object from the shell. It looked like the tall trunk of a tree, but it had no leaves, only two branches at the top. They all toiled together to drag the thing up the hill, which rises from the rocks to far above the dunes and bushes. We watched in awe, for it had long been a sacred place to us, marked untellable years before by one of our wandering tribes with a cairn: one of the innumerable graves of our savior hero, the hunter Heitsi-Eibib, who had died many times, yet never died. What sacrilege were these intruders about to commit? We were trembling in anger and trepidation as we watched the strange men opening up a deep hole among the rocks of our cairn. Into this pit they lowered their bare tree, then carefully steadied it in place with the rocks they had removed, adding others to it, raising the mound to the height of a man.

Our fear turned to jubilation. With our own eyes we had witnessed that, far from desecrating the grave, these people also respected our Great Hunter; so there was nothing to fear anymore. There was the living proof of blessings to come: their great cross planted in our cairn.

And just after sunrise the following morning, when the seabirds once more began to lay their eggs on the water, we approached the visitors quite openly on the beach. This time it was they who seemed apprehensive. But we made a great show of laying down our arrows on one side and carried calabashes of milk to the edge of the water, which seemed to dispel their doubts.

The problem was that it was impossible to talk to the visitors. I had the distinct impression that they knew nothing resembling a language. They could utter sounds, but these were quite meaningless, like the chattering of birds. So perhaps they were a kind of bird after all. However, we tried to communicate with them through gestures and after a while they began to respond in the same way. What really won us over was when some of them turned back to the eggshells on the beach and brought from them the skins and knives and vessels we'd left among the rocks the day we'd run away in such haste. Moreover, they offered us *tawete,* the gifts strangers bring in greeting to those they meet on their way. The most beautiful shiny beads in all colors, and lengths of copper, and clothing that made our womenfolk burst into laughter, and stuff to chew and smoke that drew water from the inside of our cheeks. And something else, too, which I find it difficult to talk about, a kind of fiery water that set one's insides ablaze, a magic liquid incomparably stronger than any fermented milk or honey beer one could imagine.

Difficult to talk about, I say, because at the very first taste of it, noticing how it caused my people to start cavorting, I realized that this spelled danger. And even more so when later in the day I discovered that an unfamiliar madness had taken possession of many among us. No matter what I said to them, all they could do in reply was to grin stupidly at me, quite incapable of speech or movement.

This thing needs watching, I warned them that evening. There's something behind this. It's a way of softening us up. Tomorrow, if those men come back with their firewater, we must refuse to drink. Anything else we might accept, but not this.

They dutifully agreed. But the next day I discovered that no one was paying any attention to me. Meek and mild when they knew I was watching, but the moment I turned away they let go. No doubt about the cause either. One could smell it at a distance, and their outbursts of hilarity were an ample giveaway. And when I took my *kierie* to them, there was a sound of angry bees coming from them, the first sign of insubordination they had ever shown. Why did I want to deny them something as good as that? they asked. You'll soon find out, I said; except by then it will be too late.

During that long day it became clear that the strangers were interested in more than offering gifts: they wanted something in exchange. And the first thing they wanted was women. One doesn't need language to explain that; there are signs anyone can understand. All right, I agreed, if the bride price was acceptable. But soon I discovered, to my disgust, that several of my men, once they'd gorged themselves on firewater, were offering their women and daughters for free. I tried to stop a few of the older men, but it was like sheep breaking from a *kraal*—a few here, a few there, then suddenly a stream tearing past you on all sides.

Something curious I noticed, even through my anger. Those strangers who had bought women first took them to the fresh water. Not to wash them from head to toe as one might expect (and perhaps that was just as well, for water is a precious thing and not to be wasted on washing), but only a few drops spattered on their faces while the men mumbled something and touched their own foreheads and chests and shoulders. Looked as if they were giving names to the women. Which was ridiculous, as they already had names. All of these new names, I now recall in retrospect, were Mary-this or Mary-that. And as soon as a woman was named she was taken away into the bushes. Then came the funniest bit: as the newlyweds returned the men gave back the women. At first we were offended, especially those among us who'd received a good bride price; then we discovered that the strangers did not want a refund. Each time they took a woman to the bushes they paid the price anew. A man could get rich like that.

Only, I remained worried about the firewater. Even more

so when the strangers began to intimate that they wanted sheep too. A woman is one thing, but sheep and goats and cattle are something else. The moment we were alone again I spoke to my crowd with great urgency. All right, I said, we can offer a handful of sheep at the highest possible price, but then no more.

But the very next day I came upon some of my people, some of the best ones, too, men like Sigeb and Aob and Daghab, surreptitiously driving a whole flock from the kraal to the beach. From the way the herdsmen were high-stepping behind the sheep it was clear that they'd been plied with firewater again; and when I tried to prevent them, Sigeb came stumbling toward me, brandishing his kierie, can you believe it? It was easy enough to fell him, but some of the others I couldn't stop. I had no choice but to go down to the beach to talk to the strangers myself, if one can call it talking: to ask for my sheep back. Instead of reacting in the friendly manner of the previous days they became quite menacing. One of them grabbed a kind of iron kierie and before I knew what was happening the thing emitted a thunderclap right beside me, which sent me sprawling. From that I knew for sure that, in spite of their first appearances, these people had nothing to do with Heitsi-Eibib, they were an evil lot, a bunch of cheats, undoubtedly followers of Gaunab's, straight from his Black Heaven.

Once more, that evening, I spoke to my assembled people, to persuade them that there was trouble coming. To my dismay some of them rose up and told me to shut up: they were no longer listening to me. One of them, Khusab of all people, my childhood friend, spoke while openly clutching a *karba* of firewater in his hand. Where did you get that? I asked him. None of your business, he told me. I jumped at him and grabbed the karba; but when I turned round there was a half-moon of people waiting with their kieries. I was ready to dash that pot to pieces on the nearest rock; but Khusab said: "You break that thing, you get broken too." And some of the others said: "Give it back." As I stood glowering at them, angry as a lizard, they took the karba from me and began to pass it from one to the other, each man taking a big gulp while staring straight into my eyes. The audacity. Next morning they were sprawled out all over the place, a disgusting sight, snoring away like animals, while I sat there aching inside, mourning for a thing that was breaking among us.

For the next few days I had to avoid them. A few of the older men were beginning to see things my way, I am happy to say, but the younger ones were troublesome. And who knows what might yet have happened if I hadn't found the woman just then.

You may well ask me what a woman was doing on those ships. It is a question that has often plagued me in my later lives. Nowhere have I found any evidence that da Gama or Cam or Dias or d'Almeida or any other seafarer of the time took along women on their ships or brought them home from elsewhere. On the contrary, such a practice would have run counter to all social, economic, moral, religious, or pragmatic considerations of the time. On the other hand, precisely because such considerations existed, one can expect that had such women been aboard senhor da Gama and his colleagues would have done everything in their considerable power to conceal the fact. Not so? And even if they did set sail from the mouth of the Tagus with no female on board, what would have prevented them from picking up some along the way?—the wives of preachers or tradesmen, castaways, slaves, or whatever? In any case it hardly matters what history records. The simple fact is that on this particular voyage, in the midst of all those outlandish men, there *was* a woman. And I found her.

On the morning of the sixth day she was hatched from an egg deposited on the waves by one of the great seabirds, which still lay brooding on the waters in the dark blue distance.

2

A *small chapter about a big misunderstanding*

She was alone. High up on the rocky hill where they had planted the cross I sat watching the brown egg coming slowly toward the land until she emerged from it and got out on the hard wet sand. It was still early dawn when I had gone up the hill with my goatskin bag filled with gifts for Heitsi-Eibib: a calabash of honey, an ostrich egg brought all the way from Camdebo, sour milk, goat fat, a small bag of *buchu*. Let those treacherous strangers do what they wish, I thought, I would rededicate this place to Heitsi-Eibib in the proper way.

It was a bad time for me. One mind in my head told me I was being too hard on my people, the strangers really meant well; but another mind said no, they were acting like a jackal taking over an aardvark's hole. To and fro in my head these thoughts were going, this way and that, this way and that, night and day. Which was why I had gone up there so early, to where I would be left in peace, staring out across the wide shell of the bay where we came to spend our summers. Behind me was the land, green and dense but angry, with its thorn thickets and its rock beds, vultures and *koo* birds in the sky, the humps and carbuncles of its mountains, dark secret streams running in the earth below; in front of me the cold sea, streaked with white. Soon after I took up my position I saw the eggs of the great birds coming out to the land. Down below my people were waiting for them. Today they would go hunting. I had warned them not to trust the *k'onkwas,* the Beard Men, but who still heeded me? I saw the men disappear into the underbrush as our women and children scattered slowly across the curve of the bay to the far side until they were as small as ants. I sat motionless.

That was when the single eggshell set out toward the beach, an afterthought; I'd never even seen it being laid, it just happened. Even with the wind behind it, the shell was making difficult progress, swaying and bobbing awkwardly, not moving as swiftly as the others usually did. It took a long time before it scraped over the sand and the person inside was hatched. His clothes seemed longer than those of the other men who had come from the sea before, more brightly colored too, but apart from that I didn't notice anything out of the ordinary. On bare feet, bare white feet, the person crossed the sandy beach toward the broad shallow mouth of the stream directly below my perch. He clambered unsteadily over the outcrops of rocks: I was still thinking of the person as "he." From time to time he squatted down beside a rock pool to poke around in it with a stick, prodding, it seemed, at sea urchins and purple anemones; then went a few yards further, squatted down; went on again. At length he reached the furthest edge, tall and erect, neck stretched to peer in all directions as if to make sure there was nothing and no one in sight, like a *meerkat* inspecting its surroundings. Satisfied that the place was deserted, he began to undo and peel off layer upon layer upon layer of clothing, down to the white core, like a wild *baru* bulb dug up in the veld. I remained where I was, unmoving. The bare creature down below moved cautiously along the rocks toward the long, narrow pool at the far side of the outcrop, stopping again from time to time to look about. There were only the gulls. And I; but the stranger could not see me, not where I was hunched up among the rocks. I waited until after he had lowered himself into the pool before I came down the hill. Still not suspecting anything.

It was only when I reached the very edge of the rock pool that I discovered it was not a man at all but a woman. Those round calabashes, that small thatched mound, no man could mistake them. In the same instant she caught sight of me and uttered a scream. I quickly reached down to pick up her clothing, meaning to offer them to her, but that really worked her up. Like a crab she scuttled awkwardly to the far side of the pool, stumbling with every step, stopping from time to time to splash jets of white water in my direction. I couldn't understand her fright at all. Hadn't I made it obvious that I meant her no harm?

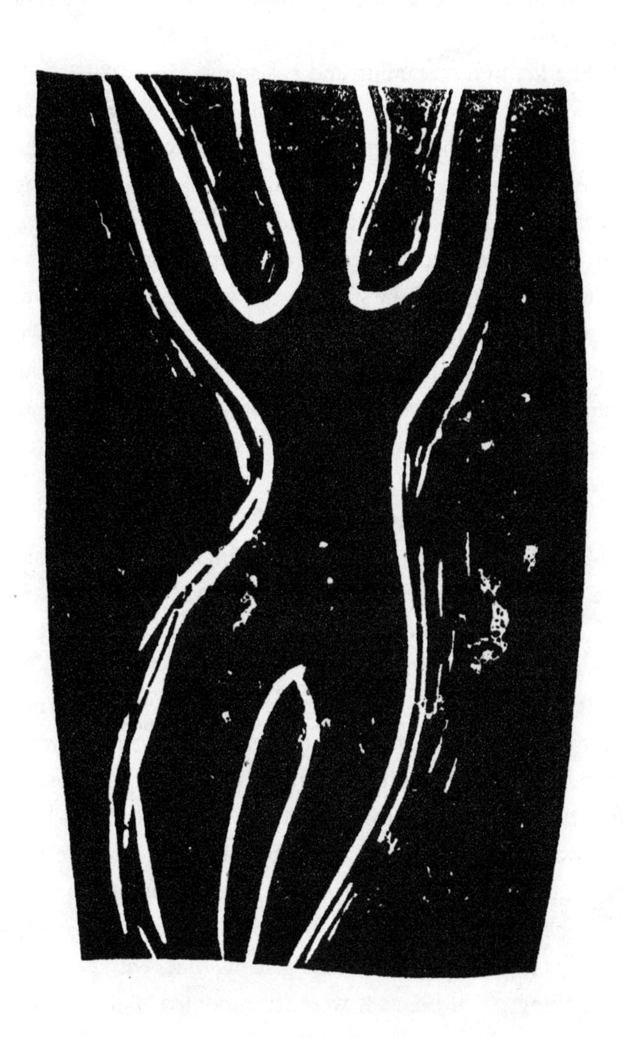

"Mutsi atse," I greeted her politely, the way I was brought up to do. "I see you."

She kept on screaming and splashing.

To prove to her my peaceful intentions, to show her I was not hiding anything which might harm her, I undid the thongs of the *ghai* apron of soft musk-cat skin I was wearing to cover my honorable parts. The yell she uttered then was ear-splitting, something terrifying. Jumped right out of the water, slipping along the smooth rock surfaces, falling down, scuttling on all fours, getting up again, down and up, down and up, in a wide half-moon across the beach, following the line of the high tide where the sand was firm, away from me, back to where she had been hatched, squawking all the time like a gull gone mad.

"Hebba ha!" I shouted after her. "Come back!"

But her long white legs kept on swinging out as she ran, the way a woman runs, her long dark hair streaming after her, until at last, head over heels, she tumbled back into the egg that had brought her to the shore.

It was like one of those dreams the night walkers bring on to trouble a man in his sleep: when you wake up your member stands rearing up and trembling like a mamba ready to strike. And immediately I realized what had scared her, the way others had been scared before her, ever since the girl-and-boy games of our youth when it was becoming obvious what I, T'kama Big Bird, had inherited from my unruly father. If only she would give me time: with patience everything could be, as it were, surmounted. But patience was the one thing I, too, lacked just then. Because I knew only too well, as I stood there staring at her and trembling, that I had been struck to the quick by an arrow daubed with bitter-berry magic. This rearing mamba in my loins—erect like the tall cross now planted in Heitsi-Eibib's sacred cairn—would not know any peace again before it had come to rest deep in the *kloof* made for it. Dejected and sad as I was, I did not even try to follow her. Just stood there watching her grow small in the distance as she ran across the copper beach back to her egg and started striking into the low surf, further and further away from me, right out of my life, forever, into the dark green sea.

In which flows the first blood of this story

Not quite, though, and not entirely into the dark green sea, for what would have remained then for me to tell? So for the sake of my story, for the sake of the whole history still ahead of us at this point, I shall bring her back to the land. It may have been the wind that was too strong; or perhaps she simply lacked the strength to keep rowing against the swell of the incoming tide. But even if she had been capable, I would have written her back to the beach today.

As I stood there watching from the rocks (almost washed away myself by the new tide, to which I paid scant attention), as I sit here hauling in that dancing boat from wave to wave, from line to line, tugging, scribbling, she was brought back, back to the copper beach, where the sea spat her out a second time. But she made no move to leave the dark shell that held her. Bunched into a small heap inside she lay, a naked chicken in its broken egg. Until it struck me that perhaps what she had against me was that I had picked up her clothes; perhaps she'd thought I wanted to steal them. So I decided to prove to her my good intentions. The huts were too far away for me to fetch from there what I needed: who knows what might happen to her if I turned my back? This is the only excuse I can advance today for the sacrilege I felt driven to commit that morning—in the ardent hope, though, that Heitsi-Eibib, who had himself been a man of many women, his innumerable children scattered across the continent before he started dying and rising again, would understand my desperation and would look on my solution with understanding, if not with open approval.

I tied on my brief ghai apron again and then, still clutching the woman's clothes, hurried up the rocky ridge. When I stopped for breath halfway up the incline, I noticed that she was watching my every move; but she quickly ducked away behind the rim of the shell when she saw me looking back. That reassured me somewhat. She was human after all, and curious like the rest of us. No doubt about her womanness. At the top of the hill, below the cross, I picked up the offerings I'd left there earlier—there were ants crawling in the honey, but the rest was fine, the ostrich egg from Camdebo, the buchu in the small bag, the goat fat and curdled milk—asking Heitsi-Eibib's pardon for robbing him like that, but promising solemnly that I would replace my sacrifice the very next morning. Then down the hill again toward the ever more turbulent foam churning about the brown hull of the shell on the beach.

The whole bundle of offerings retrieved from Heitsi-Eibib's grave, wrapped in her bronze-colored top dress, I held out to the woman, explaining at the same time that as soon as her menfolk returned I would offer them a full bride price for her. But of all my talk she appeared to understand as little as her companions had before; and if my ghai apron hadn't still been straining with urgency, I might well have given up trying to communicate with a woman from a tribe that didn't even possess the power of speech. Round and round the shell I moved, trying to catch a glimpse of her face, but she kept on ducking out of sight. So in the end I decided that if language proved fruitless I should try another approach. I began to coo like a dove, I called like a *bokmakierie,* twittered like a weaver bird, warbled like a *piet-my-vrou;* I imitated the cries of the jackal and hyena, I grumbled like a lion. But she paid no attention. Kept on turning her head away. Until, at my wits' end, I cautiously laid a hand on her shoulder to calm her down. Which turned out to be the wrong decision, for she uttered another of her shrieks and grabbed the rowing-stick that was lying on the floor of her shell and started belaboring my head and shoulders.

It wasn't just because this annoyed me, but because I knew there is only one remedy for a woman in that state, that I snatched the rowing-stick from her hands and gave her a swipe to the side of her head.

She made a moaning sound, and fell down.

No matter what I did, I couldn't bring her around again.

The only solution was to revive her with fresh water. I heaved her on my shoulder and carried her past the rocks to the mouth of the stream, where I laid her gently in the cold water, her head on the bank. I'd never seen anything quite as beautiful as that, and from close by too. Almost involuntarily my hands followed the path of my eyes to convince themselves that she was really true, this smooth creature, this woman.

That was how they found me, the hunters, when they returned from the bush. At first I thought it was their way of shouting greetings when I heard them screaming from a distance, and I gleefully waved back at them, laughing with joy, taking in one hand the thing that was standing all by itself so that they could see my intentions were honorable, considering that by that time they'd been to the bushes with so many of our women.

But to my amazement I heard once more that thunderclap coming from a clear sky, seeing at the same time smoke wafting from the mouth of one of their kieries; I felt a jerking movement in my arm and suddenly I was covered in blood.

It is difficult, five hundred years later, to give a clear account of what happened. A matter of memory. We had never seen guns or shooting before, remember. Those of us who'd gone with the hunters had witnessed something of it earlier in the day, as they reported later; but I'd been waiting innocently on the beach, so I had no idea at all of what had happened when the ball struck me. That it could have been much worse I realized afterward when I was told how Khusab, remembering what had happened to springbok and wildebeest on the hunt, had tried to snatch the gun away from the leader of the expedition just as he was taking aim. Khusab, the son of T'kuni, the son of Gaun, whose mother had been one of the San. The two of us, as I have said before, he and I, had grown up together, had dug out tubers and roots and wild onions together—*baru* and *kambro* and *njaba*—had learned together to shoot arrows and make fire and herd sheep, had hunted together, had hidden side by side at the edge of the clay pit to spy on the giggling girls as they stretched the inner lips of their entrances to form lobes as long and red as the gills of a wild cock, a sight for a man's eyes to revel in, and silky to the touch. When the strangers had first begun to barter, offering us their pernicious firewater, Khusab had led the revolt against me as I have already, sadly, told. But on that day it was he who saved my life.

From the moment that first shot died away there was turmoil on the beach. Some of the k'onkwa started shooting blindly with their guns, while our men retaliated with bows and arrows; some of them picked up stones to throw—that reflex still seen in our townships half a millennium later; others tore into the strangers to wrestle them to the ground. The whole beach was teeming with shouting, fighting bodies. A thunderstorm of shots, five or six of our people tumbling down, their bodies jerking and twitching in the contortions of death; while two of the Beard Men fell under our stones. I shouted at Khusab. With two or three of the others he came running to me to give a hand with the naked woman, who was by now scratching and biting and thrashing about to get back to her people. We dragged her off to the thickets beyond the dunes while the din of the battle raged on. More shots, more men falling. It was as if Gaunab the Black One himself had been let loose among us. And all the while blood was streaming down my shoulder until I was red from head to toe.

From the far side of the bay our women and children had heard the noise and came running home. That was when it really went dark inside me, for I saw the strangers taking aim at them too. Several of them fell down, small children among them, and there was nothing at all we could do to stop them.

We scurried into the bushes, dragging the wild woman with us. If those Beard Men had known anything about tracking there would have been little hope for us; we left a spoor of broken branches and blood and drag marks as far as we went. But they were either stupid or scared, or both. We were forced after a while to tie up the woman's mouth with thongs, though it made my heart contract to see her like that—didn't she realize I meant her no harm?—and at last her moaning stopped.

Deep into the euphorbia forest we went, not daring to go near the huts, as the k'onkwa already knew that route by heart; until at last it seemed safe to call a halt so that old Khamab could attend to me. He was our *t'gai aob̆,* our wise old medicine man, who could converse as easily with the *Sobo khoin,* the People of the Shadows, as with us. He was older than any tortoise, and there was nothing he didn't know. The blood that was still flowing from the wound he caught in the horn of a buck. For fear that the k'onkwa's poison in the wound might be as bad as that of a snake, he pounded a dried lizard and mixed that with thornwood ash to rub into the wound, then sealed it up with goat fat sprinkled with finely rubbed dried leaves. Into a calabash of water he stirred ground porcupine intestines, which he forced me to drink.

Only then did he speak, softly, so that no one else could hear, his voice rough and grumbling with contained anger.

"Why did you bring the woman?"

"I want her."

"She is not one of us."

"I must have her."

"Have you seen the evil you brought on us today? Isn't that enough for you yet, T'kama?"

"Khamab, I know it is a terrible thing that has happened. But I must have her. Tsui-Goab sent her to me."

"Who are you to take Tsui-Goab's name so lightly on your lips?"

"I know it was He."

"And suppose this isn't the end of it? Suppose it is just a beginning?"

"She's mine, Khamab. I cannot give her up now."

"This may be a thing of blood and years."

"So be it then. I must have her."

Still grumbling under his breath, he left me. At the other side of the fire, where the darkness began, I saw the woman sitting on the ground, leaned back against a trunk. The food the other women brought her she hadn't touched with hand or mouth. Just sat there staring into the fire.

"Khois," I whispered. "Woman."

She didn't look up. Perhaps she hadn't even heard me.

"*Khois*." More loudly this time.

Still no movement. There I was, at this side of the fire, rampant with desire. But it was more than desire. An urge to be with her, forever, through days and years of the heat of summer and the cold of winter, hard earth, springbok stampedes, dust, clay, illness and suffering and the birth of children, moon dances and the monotonous drone of the gurah, plains, mountains, bushes, day and night, life and death.

I touched my shoulder. The bleeding had stopped. But there was something in me knew that old Khamab had been right. This was not the end of the blood.

4

In which an answer is given to a question which must have been smoldering in the reader's mind for some time now, to wit: Given the anxious circumstances in which they spent that night, the emotional condition of the woman from the sea, the nature of the narrator's wound and the size of his member—did he have intercourse with her?

No.

5

In which a solution to a tricky situation is temporarily postponed while the narrator proceeds to describe the decisive events of the following day

Dazed from lack of sleep, we got up the next morning, knowing we had to make preparations for what lay ahead. Before the day was out the matter of the Beard Men, the k'onkwa, would have to be settled one way or another. There was not much talk in our ranks. I could easily have reproached my people for not having heeded my warnings from the beginning by keeping away from the strangers; but then, not without justification, they might just as easily have replied that nothing had gone wrong before I had become involved with the woman. It was better for all of us to concentrate, not on what lay behind us, but on what was to be done.

As it happened, the matter was resolved much more easily than anyone had ever expected. A few of our men, sent out to survey the beach, returned to report that the strangers were burying their dead. Soon after came word that they were on their way to our huts, each man with his thunderstick. The women broke into loud wails and ululations when they heard the news, but I ordered them to be silent. Leaving the white woman to their care, with a small band of older men for their protection, the rest of us moved swiftly into the bushes along the narrow path to the beach. The rest was almost ludicrously easy. An arrow shot from the bush makes no sound at all: by the time you notice it your legs are already buckling and you are left with a burning spot in your back, or wherever it struck you. The first man did not even cry out. Perhaps that increased their fear. The second, hit with less accuracy, began to scream like a wounded baboon. Some of the others were ready to turn tail, and their leaders had to prod them forward with their guns. But after the fourth there was a stampede back to the beach.

My men were eager to ransack the bodies of the fallen, but I stopped them. Not a patch of foreign cloth, not a span of copper, not a feather from a hat should ever be seen in our midst again.

Khusab and I remained behind to keep watch; the others returned to the huts. From behind the front row of dunes we saw the shells rowing a few hundred yards into the sea, where they drew in the sticks, bobbing about in silence as if they couldn't make up their minds about coming or going. Only after a very long time, when the sun had already passed us overhead, two of the boats came back. Warily the Beard Men began to cross the beach. Khusab wanted us to call in our men again, but I held him back. The two of us were enough. We remained hidden in the underbrush close to the path, in which the seamen proceeded with great caution, stopping in their tracks every few yards to check the surroundings. It was soon evident that they had come to collect the bodies of their fallen comrades. But just to make sure they would never return to our coast we shot a few arrows into the sand the moment they reached the beach again, staggering under the weight of their dead. This time we did not mean to kill them, only to warn them that we were watching. They got the message.

After they had rowed off I sent Khusab to call our people. We were all assembled on the beach when the four great waterbirds in the distance puffed up their billowing white feathers and slowly sailed away. The woman was with us, her ankles tied together. As the birds moved away she crumpled wretchedly into a small bundle on the sand. I kneeled beside her and untied her legs.

"You can stay with us now," I told her.

She made no movement.

"I won't do you any harm," I assured her. "All I want is for you to be with me. You're mine now."

She still made no movement.

The others began to bury our dead. It was no pleasant task as the vultures had been there before us. The first they went for were the children, one of them a baby in an abba skin.

All the while I remained beside the woman, until the work was done. The others were preparing to go home. I motioned to them to go, the woman wouldn't try to escape any longer. For a long time after they had left I tried to comfort her and raise her spirits, but she didn't even seem to be aware of my presence.

In the late afternoon, both dejected and annoyed, I took her back to our place and handed her over to the women. All by myself I returned to the beach, and in the red glow of the sunset I went up the hill to Heitsi-Eibib's cairn, where I left new gifts for the great hunter.

One could still make out, if you stared very keenly and used a bit of imagination, four dark specks in the furthest distance of the sea, disappearing sometimes behind the swell, then appearing once more, then gone again. On the beach the tide rose slowly and meticulously, covering with foam the tracks of the people who had been there, the dragging marks of the dead, until nothing at all remained. It was as if my world had been restored to me. The strangeness had been peeled away. Still and brimful the sea lay before me, as calm as the face of a woman telling a lie.

6

In which the day breaks

Looking back across five centuries I find it hard to recall a particular morning, and I cannot guarantee that it was then as I'm telling it now. But here is my attempt, with the advantages of hindsight:

I can see myself sitting there throughout the night, leaning against the bare trunk the seamen had planted in Heitsi-Eibib's cairn, my wounded shoulder growing painful in the severe night cold, throbbing with angry life, drooping like the broken wing of a bird. The stars passing overhead, the upside-down moon, the glowing embers of *Tsaob* stretched across the sky. In the predawn the twittering in the thickets, and in the first streak of light a row of black geese in the gray sky. They must have noticed that winter was setting in. Of the seabirds that had brought the Beard Men to our shore there was no sight at all. Not a single footprint in the sand. A bushbuck barking beyond the first euphorbias. For the rest, only me sitting there, caught in the great fist of the land.

The woman. I'm thinking about the woman. When I get up from here, soon, she will be there, mine now. We have passed the moment when choice was possible. Yesterday I might have let her go, I might have decided to return her to her people. (Would they have taken her back? But that was part of something else.) I could have let her go and freed myself of her. Now she is there. Now I have taken up the burden of her existence in my conscience—this is how I register it now, whether or not I was fully conscious of it then—and with her, so much more besides: generations, and faith, and violence, an entire future, life, war, hope.

We cannot stay here. This shore has been violated. We must pack up and trek away into the remote interior.

An early-morning breeze has sprung up. I can feel the hill yielding to its gentle insistence, can feel us drifting slowly through space, the hill with its single arm stump outstretched, I with my drooping wing, traveling into the day, high above the lapping sea. It is as if the world is changed into song, not the twittering of birds or the *hadedas* waking up or the geese squawking, not the gulls, but the world itself singing in its deepest darkest voice, a rumble deeper than the roar of lions or the thundering hooves of trekking wildebeest, a singing of the earth and its rocks and hills and thickets and mountains, from throat and mouth and intestines and bones and rampant cocks and the secret depths of women, a rumble ringing in my own ears. Listening to it I accept my land, I sing my land, in my tongue and throat I give it sound, I name it. I say: wood, and turn to wood. I say:

mountain, hill, rock, river, sea, and become each of them in turn. I say lion, jackal, mockingbird, partridge, *kiewiet,* I say *kombro,* I say *dagga,* I say *kierie* and *kaross,* I say *khuseti,* I say *t'gau,* I say *k'hrab,* I say *k'arakup,* I say beetle and fly and field mouse, I say vulture and carrion, sun and moon, day and night, Tsui-Goab and Gaunab, I say creature, I say man, I say woman. I say future unfolding, horizons breaking, trees exploding, suns erupting from rocks, women giving birth to monsters and giants, fishes playing the *t'koi-t'koi,* guinea fowl snaring antelopes, snakes carrying firestones on their forehead, Heitsi-Eibib dying time and time again and rising every time from stone, I say plains turning into flesh, I say blood and bleeding, I fill the day with names, I inscribe the plains like a sheet of paper, I say laughter, I say weeping, I say death and birth, I say gazelles in a calabash and ostriches in curdled milk, I say falling stars and chameleons and hares with split upper lips and lice carrying messages from the waning moon and water snakes devouring themselves and fat-tailed sheep sailing upside down through the sky. I say everything that is still to happen and everything no one has ever thought up, I say a terrible I and a fearsome you, and in the sound of my own shout I walk into the day that breaks open before me like an egg from which impossible new words are hatched.

7

In which fine feathers fail to make a fine bird

The others were already making preparations for the trek when I reached our encampment. No one had discussed it beforehand: like the migrating geese we all simply knew, simultaneously, that we could not remain in a place where such things had happened. The land lay waiting for us, and it was vast.

All the way down the rocky hill, across the beach and over the dunes and along the path through the undergrowth—here and there on the slopes of low hills the aloes already beginning to glow red-hot as if preparing to set the place on fire—I was worrying about the woman. How would I ever tame her? She was clearly wild with fear. Another direct approach was out of the question after she'd taken to her heels the very first time I had undone my ghai apron.

(And to think I'd done it only to reassure her, perhaps to impress her: was it not the greatest compliment a man could pay a woman?)

If only I could explain to her: but the woman couldn't speak. Then I remembered the birdlike sounds her Beard Men used to utter, and that set me thinking about birds. What with those exorbitant colorful clothes they had worn, and she too when she'd been with them, they resembled birds more than any other live thing I had seen. Which was why I hatched the thought that perhaps one could tame her by following the example of her kind. Only, they were gone by now, so how would I discover their rituals of mating? I had seen them naming the women they had acquired from us before coupling with them, and that I was prepared to do, but would it be enough?

As I wandered along the narrow winding path where the day before we had attacked the strangers with our arrows, I came upon the hat of one of the k'onkwa in a white-thorn bush. Yesterday I'd forbidden my people to lay their hands on a single bead or hair or feather of the intruders; but this was a different matter. I tore the hat from the bush, and dusted it, and twirled it on my hand to study it from all sides. The shiny buckle, the frivolous tail plume. And it occurred to me that if I put on that hat I would resemble the men of her own kind, and that might persuade her to go down and turn her docile tail to me the way female birds do to their prancing males.

The others drew back when they saw me coming into the opening in the bush, not recognizing me at first. But in a moment they did. By that time the cattle skins had already been peeled from some of the huts and rolled into bundles, leaving the bare latticework like unfinished or abandoned nests.

"Good," I said. "The sun must not set on us in this place again."

"We'll be on our way before the sun is high," said old Khamab through the bluish fumes of his dagga pipe. He made a motion with his gray head to draw me closer, and asked softly, out of earshot of the others: "But what about the woman?"

"What about her?"

"You leaving her here, or what?"

"How can I leave her here? She is mine. She is coming with."

"The people will complain. She is not one of us."

"It is my woman. They'll get used to her."

"You haven't even managed to *kwekwa* her yet."

"How do you know?"

He grinned, baring his toothless tortoise gums, turning his watery eyes to the sun. "I know everything."

I squatted down beside him. "Khamab, there's no need for you to worry. Before we leave this place it will have been done."

"It's high day."

"If one unrolls the doorskin of a hut closed it is night inside."

He clicked his tongue. "The things of day and night must be kept apart."

"There's time enough. I'll ask the women to prepare her."

He said nothing, but the way he blew out smoke was

eloquent enough. He was still sitting there when I came back from the women, turning round to watch them as they entered the hut where the smooth-haired woman was kept. I knew the ritual. They would grease her body with goat fat from head to toe; then rub fragrant buchu powder into her limbs, in every fold and cranny. That was our custom. And while they were busy inside the hut—one could hear the murmuring of their voices, occasionally broken by a sudden shrill burst of laughter—old Khamab helped me to prepare myself. I was resolved to make an unforgettable impression. The plumed hat I drew down over my head, almost covering my eyes, so that I had to walk with my head thrown back in order to see. Then flowers. Plastered into the grease with which I had thickly covered my whole body. Small blue and yellow and white ones, covering every square inch of my skin. And into the coarse hair at the bottom of my belly I plaited the blood-red petals from aloes. What with all this activity and thinking about what lay ahead, the thing was already standing up mightily again, and that gave me the idea of tying to it the biggest, whitest, most beautiful ostrich feather I could find among our bundles. You should have seen that feather quivering with every step I took. The flowers kept on falling off as I moved about, but there were enough of them left. What woman could refuse a man like that? Look at the birds: weaver birds, and finches, paradise birds, hornbills, swallows: it is always the male that is most brightly plumed.

Behold the man: here I come.

The women have left the hut. I enter. Everything has become deadly quiet outside and I know they are drawing together in a tight circle around the hut to listen. Inside, too, it is absolutely still, not a breath of sound.

It takes me a long time, standing motionless, to get accustomed to the dark. At last I can see her clearly, in a small curled-up bundle opposite me, her back turned to me, anointed with smoothness, shining in her nakedness, all woman, and with that long hair.

"Khois," I say, my voice choking in my throat, and the feather shaking on its trembling mast.

I dare to come closer, shedding petals with every move, strutting in small stiff steps like a ground hornbill, following the lead of my plumed staff.

"Khois," I say again, surprised at the strangeness of my own voice. "Here I am."

A small movement of her head. Hands covering her face. But at last I see the fingers part.

I bow before her, but that causes the hat to drop right over my eyes, so I can see no more. I stamp my right foot on the dung floor to make sure she will not miss the fluttering plume. Thinking in my mind: Heitsi-Eibib, Tsui-Goab, People of the Shadows, of yesterday and tomorrow, behold me now, I feel a great thing coming.

And then she bursts out laughing.

If she'd started screaming again in fear like the first day, fine; even if she'd shouted at me in rage, or sworn at me, or begun to cry. What I would have liked best was a sound to say, "Come here." But any other reaction, even of revulsion, I could have handled. Except her laughter. And once she'd started she couldn't stop again. It was so violent that she toppled right over on the floor, and it went on for so long that it began to sound like sobbing, but it was laughter, so totally uncontrollable that her whole body was shaking.

Nothing brings a man down as quickly as laughter. In a moment that whole great proud feather was drooping limply on its bough. And still she went on laughing.

"Hurry up," I curtly told Khamab when I came outside. "We're leaving. What are you staring at? We've got a long road ahead. Haven't you ever seen a feather before?" I tore off the damn thing and trampled it into the dust; and the hat I threw whirring into the euphorbias.

And so we set out on our trek of years and droughts. And if I think back now of everything that happened before we returned to that place, my hand is almost too heavy to shape another word.

8

In which an attempt is made to reconstruct on a modern map the route presumably followed by the narrator and his tribe during their years of wandering before at last they returned to Algoa Bay (Port Elizabeth), *which might have been the place they had set out from*

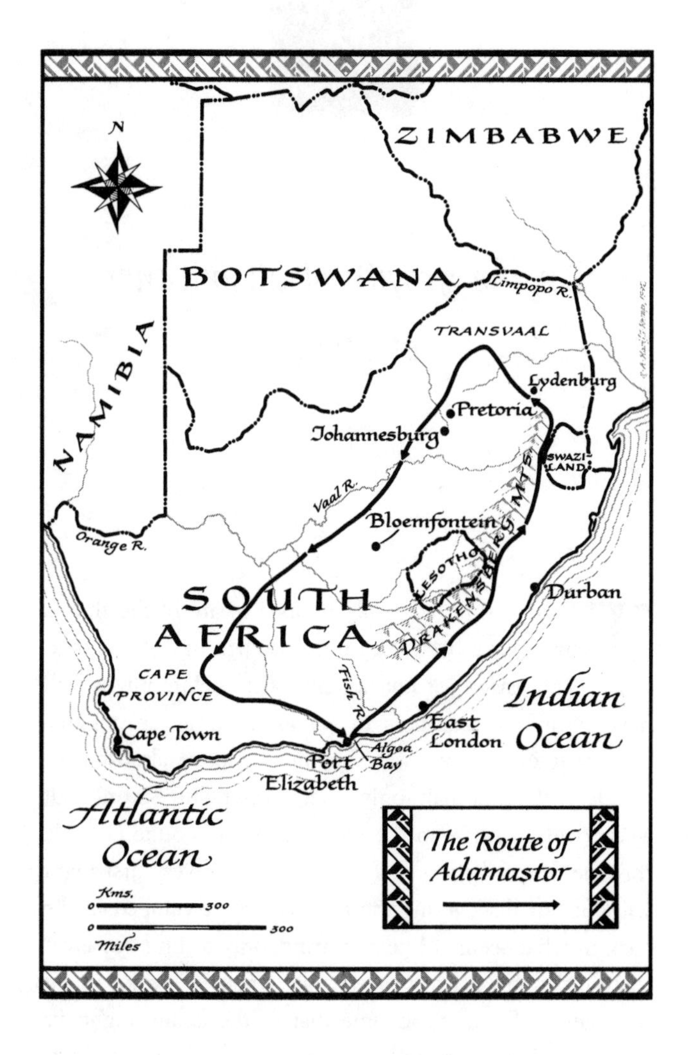
ZIMBABWE
BOTSWANA
NAMIBIA
Limpopo R.
TRANSVAAL
Lydenburg
Pretoria
Johannesburg
SWAZI-LAND
Vaal R.
Bloemfontein
Orange R.
LESOTHO
DRAKENSBERG MTS.
Durban
SOUTH AFRICA
CAPE PROVINCE
Fish R.
Indian Ocean
East London
Cape Town
Algoa Bay
Port Elizabeth
Atlantic Ocean
The Route of Adamastor
Kms.
0
300
0
300
Miles

9

On the growth of all manner of things

The first time we really became aware of the thorns must have been the third or fourth day of our trek. The reason for not noticing them before might well have been our eagerness to get as far away as possible from that evil place: we were on the move almost constantly, calling a halt only after sunset and setting out again before sunrise in the morning. So it is quite possible that the thorns had been growing from the very first night without our discovering the fact. When we camped in the dark in what seemed like a clearing, only to find ourselves surrounded by dense thornbushes when we woke up, it was natural for us to assume that in the falling night we simply hadn't taken proper notice of our surroundings.

But on that particular day it was impossible to ignore the phenomenon.

The day before we had been so exhausted that we'd made a stop quite early beside a stream where the parched sheep and cattle could drink and graze their fill; and we'd been unanimous about allowing ourselves a day of rest. When at last we crawled from our bedding of grass and scrub, the sun already high in the morning sky—which was hardly our custom, as we believed that a person should be up and about before the sun can cast a shadow on one's sleeping place—we found the whole clearing densely overgrown with thorn bushes. Where there had been a wide-open space the day before these bushes were now growing, taller than any one of us. The path to the drinking place, where we had been moving freely to and fro a matter of hours before, was now invisible through the undergrowth, as was the way we'd planned to go from there, and the way along which we had arrived.

"What's this?" I asked old Khamab, knowing that he was the only one among us likely to come up with an explanation.

"Never seen such a thing," he mumbled angrily. "Perhaps we didn't look properly yesterday."

"You know as well as the rest of us that this place was quite bare yesterday."

"Perhaps it's just a very fertile spot."

"Yesterday morning and the day before we also had to break our way through the thorns, but then we thought it was because of going to bed in the dark and rising before dawn."

"There must be something trying to prevent us from going on," he said, staring morosely at a line of ants urgently carrying off all the seeds and eggs from their nest.

"What could it be?"

"Don't know. Ask the land." With his sandy eyes he swept a broad swath of the landscape around us—the dull green hills billowing like buttocks, the thickets in their folds—before turning them on me, staring unblinking against the sun. "You think it may be because of the woman?"

"There's nothing wrong with the woman."

"Have you succeeded with her yet?"

"I tried, but it was the wrong time. She's *t'nau.*"

"All we can do is pack up and move on."

"But we decided to have a day of rest. The people are exhausted. So are the animals."

"It's up to you. You're the *chu'que.* But my advice is to pack up. Look, even the ants are moving on."

Which was what we did. But it took all our strength to hack our way through that tangle of thorns and shrubs; the branches actually seemed to sprout out rapidly behind us as soon as they had been lopped off. The sun was already coming down to roost by the time we'd crossed the stream and moved uphill to a barren height. Heavy clouds were gathering overhead. Strange yellowish clouds they were, an unholy color, like blood or pus filtering through darkness. And we had our hands full with the sheep and cattle, which kept on breaking back downhill toward the stream and the thickets of thorn. By nightfall we were missing several of them, so we decided to leave off until the morrow.

But that night a storm broke out, which was most unusual, for the rainy season in those parts was still months away as we knew from generations of experience. Lightning running through the sky like flaming cracks, thunder rumbling like mountains sundering or cliffs crashing. Rain pouring right through us where we sat huddled together, scared to death, on that bare slope without any shelter. Even so we were lucky, as we discovered when the rain stopped two days later and we broke out of our tangled huddle, soaked to the bone and streaming red with mud, shivering in the thin sunlight: below us, where we had camped before, there was nothing left. In an elbow of the little river the stream had burst its banks, flooding the plains, and only small tufts of bush were visible here and there above the swirling muddy water. The sheep we'd lost had disappeared entirely. Before the day was out two of the smallest children among us and an old woman had also died of exposure, and we had to bury them under mounds of stones to keep the predators away before we could continue on our trek.

The woman was still with us, covered now from head to toe with a kaross of rock-rabbit skins the other women had given her, otherwise the cold would undoubtedly have carried her off too. We were all of us dumbfounded and depressed. It had been a bad start to the trek. And it didn't get any better either. Those growing thorns continued to haunt us: every evening we would select an open spot for our encampment; the next morning when we got up it would be overgrown. Perhaps the most unnerving aspect of the situation was that no one ever dared to discuss it openly. Except for Khamab and me, when we were alone together, all pretended that nothing out of the ordinary was going on. It was simply too dangerous to throw open the flimsy kraal of our fears and allow words to come in.

Also my shoulder was playing up badly because of the cold. Old Khamab tried everything he could. In due course the visible wound was healed, but the muscles remained tense, with a dull ache lodged in them, which was to stay with me all my life.

The woman never complained. She withdrew completely, not only into her kaross but deep into herself. After her t'nau time had passed, when the women had washed and cleansed her again, and rubbed herbs and goat fat into her and prepared her, I made several more attempts to take her aside in the night: the others would all be asleep by then, except for old Khamab, who never slept, sitting unblinking beside the fire like an ancient owl. In all the years I knew him he never slept: that was because in his youth he had once passed a water hole in the veld and dared to look into the eyes of the Great Snake with the shiny stone on its forehead.

The woman never protested or resisted when I took her aside. There were no more tears left in her, I think. Nor laughter, after that first time. I never tried to bedeck myself with feathers and flowers again. Yet it never worked. It is a shameful thing to confess, but I was simply too big for her. We tried in all imaginable ways, from above, from below, from left and right, from the side, with her lying on her back or astride on me, or on hands and knees, or standing, any imaginable way. But it was like those thorn bushes: every time my kierie came near to where it so urgently desired to introduce itself, it seemed to start growing, an impossible club, a tree trunk too large and unwieldy to enter anywhere. I had the impression that the woman was actually beginning to feel sorry for me, because that wild bird-thing was growing into proportions no human being could believe. And every time I so vainly tried to enter her, it grew some more in size, in girth, in length, until I had the feeling that it was no longer I who carried it with me but that I had become a mere appendage to my bird. I had to walk with legs astride to allow it space to stand or dangle.

This was how things stood with us, and even worse, by the time we'd crossed the first series of rivers and with our cattle and our fat-tailed sheep we came across another tribe of people.

10

In which the story of a buffalo is told and a firebird takes flight

They were people we had met before, on earlier treks when we'd passed through their territory; on some occasions we had spent several moons with them before moving on. Ever since Heitsi-Eibib's time our people had been wandering through the land, following rains or the sun, in search of grazing fields or water. But those people had more or less settled in one place with their huts and their cattle and their lands, for as far back as anyone could remember. Xhosas. We usually got along well together and we understood enough of their language, they of ours, to be friends.

By the time we reached their territory they had also, they told us, become acquainted with the strange Beard Men from the sea and had bartered cattle. Naturally they were most surprised to see the white woman among us and hear her story. (But *our* story, mine and hers, was just beginning.) We spent the winter months with them, which gave us enough time to talk and discuss and ask or give advice, and speculate about the k'onkwa and the future.

There was one man among them, not quite as old as Khamab, but old enough, thin as a stick, a witch doctor. It wasn't I who sought him out, for I knew well that Khamab would disapprove; but I presume he himself, being an *igqira,* must have noticed that there was something wrong with me. He called me aside.

"From the day you first came here," he said, "you have been losing weight every day. You must have a problem."

"I won't deny it."

"Show me your problem."

I took out my problem and showed it to him.

The igqira whistled through his front teeth. "This is really a big problem." He motioned in the direction of the women. "Is it because of that woman?"

"It is."

"Tsk, tsk."

"Do you have a remedy for me?"

"It will cost you two fat-tailed sheep."

"I'll give you three, and willingly, if you can help me."

"There's nothing I cannot help you with. I am the best igqira there is."

"Then help me."

"I shall tell you a story."

"It's advice I need, not a story."

"There's no problem in the world that cannot be solved by a story."

"Then tell me."

"Listen."

And he told me what had happened in the time before time, before his people had arrived in that place, when they had still lived much further to the north and east. In those days, he said, there had been a young man in the tribe who said to his father and mother: "I want to find myself a wife, but not from our tribe."

It was a reckless, unheard-of thing to do, and they were deeply perturbed about it, but because they loved him dearly they let him go. He gathered his *lobola* cattle and set out with them, over mountains and plains, far, far away, until he reached a place where he found a number of young girls pounding grain in tall hollowed tree trunks, and one of them caused his heart to jump. Without more ado he approached the old men of the tribe and asked their permission to marry the girl. They first demanded to know when his parents would come over to discuss the matter as was their wont, but he told them that he had all his lobola with him, and he was in a hurry. And even though their hearts were heavy with misgivings, they accepted the cattle and allowed the two to go.

Before they left the girl went to her parents. "You need not send anything with me," she said, "except for the Buffalo from the Veld, the big black one that watches over our tribe."

They spoke this way and that, for what would they do without the animal? If he were to die the whole tribe would die with him. But the girl pleaded so passionately, promising to look after the Buffalo with her own life, that for her sake they let the sacred animal go. For how, they thought, would she survive without it? Who could tell what dangers lurked where her new husband was taking her?

The girl said nothing at all about the matter to her bridegroom. And the Buffalo followed them without the young man's ever discovering his presence. In the bundle on her back the young woman had a bunch of herbs, a knife, a calabash of goat fat.

In her husband's village she was received by her in-laws with much hospitality, and the very first evening the bridegroom went to show her the fields she would be working on the morrow. She said nothing, but back in their hut the bride pretended she had lost her beads and left to look for them. In the deepening twilight she returned to the fields and found the Buffalo waiting there. Whispering, she told him what he was to do. And from that day on the villagers were amazed by her prowess. Early in the morning when the women went down to the fields hers were already plowed and sown and harvested. When they needed water she would put her pots and calabashes outside in the evening, and the next morning they would be filled to the brim. Only, she never had time to put out food for the Buffalo as her parents had always done at home. And so the animal began to waste away with hunger and thirst. When he could not bear it any longer, he complained to her one evening as she came out with her calabashes. "You may graze in the fields," she told him. "But be careful, make sure no one notices."

For a few days everything went well, but soon the villagers began to notice that something was amiss with their crops. And when they went to investigate they found buffalo tracks. Without saying anything to the women the men took their assegais and set out on a hunt. But the young woman happened to be outside and from the anxious twittering of the birds she knew that there was trouble coming. Before her mother-in-law could prevent it she ran out after the men, over the veld and through the bushes. She arrived just in time to see her husband's assegai piercing the Buffalo's head behind the right ear. The animal fell down dead. She dared not say a word for fear they would discover the truth. But after they had dismembered the Buffalo she carried the head home in her basket. There she withdrew into her hut, and nicked the Buffalo's ear, holding a horn ready to catch the blood. As the blood began to run she poured her herbs into a pot of boiling water, and with the brew she bathed the animal's wounds, singing all the while:

"O my father, Buffalo of the Plains,
They told me you would go through deep waters,
They told me you would walk through the shadows,
You are the green plant among the stones,
You make the earth fertile and cause the trees to
bear fruit,
O Buffalo of the Plains!"

And as she sang the Buffalo's head began to grow a new body, and its dull eyes were quickened with bright new life.

But before he was fully revived the woman's husband came to look for her, and when his voice was heard outside the Buffalo closed his eyes again and the heavy head rolled over the floor.

For two nights, for three nights, she repeated the spell, but each time her husband arrived before the Buffalo had been restored to life. By then it was too late. On the morning of the fourth day she asked the villagers to leave her alone so that she could bathe herself in a river pool. Shaking their heads about her strange customs, they let her be. And once she had reached the pool she went on walking and walking, over the mountains and across the plains, all the way back to her home, where she told the people what had happened. They sent out messengers to all the surrounding villages, and when the people began to arrive the young woman's husband was among them.

"What are you doing here?" she asked him. "You have killed us all."

"I don't understand it," he said. "Please explain this thing to me."

She gave no answer. All the people thronged around her, and one by one they said:

"You have gone through deep waters."

"You have walked through the shadows."

"You were the green plant among the stones."

"You made the earth fertile and caused the trees to bear fruit."

And every time, as one of them said this, whether man or woman, the one who had spoken would take a knife and plunge it into his or her own heart. Until all the people were dead. The young bride was the last to die.

The brokenhearted young man turned around and walked away from the carnage, over the mountains and across the plains, back to his own tribe. And there they said to him: "We told you not to look for a bride in a strange land but to choose one from among your own people. Now you have lost your lobola."

"I have come to you for help," I told the igqira when he had finished the tale, "and all you can offer me is a story."

"Bring me the sheep first," he said with a sigh, as if he found it hard to speak.

Once I had obeyed he seemed more satisfied. "There are two kinds of medicine," he said. "One is for you, the other for the woman. I will start with you."

We sent the woman to wait in her hut so that he could first anoint me with the salve he had prepared with his own hands, according to his wisdom. But even before he had finished it began to burn so fiercely that I felt my bird was ready to fly up into the night skies with me. I could not stop myself. Right through the fire I ran—only the next day did I discover the blisters on my feet—out of the door, through the bushes, down to the water. But it was no use. My member was burning like a log. In the end I plastered it thickly with clay to cool it off, but the clay started bubbling like boiling water, and in the moonlight I could see a cloud of steam rising from my loins. Within minutes the whole village was assembled around me to find out why I was bellowing so wildly. But I did not answer. That night I spoke in languages that had not yet been invented.

If only the cure had helped, I would still have regarded it as worth the agony. But I swear that by the following dawn, when the fire finally subsided, the thing had grown even thicker and longer than before.

In the meantime, while I was wallowing in the burning mud, the igqira had set to work on the woman. What cure he tried on her I never found out, but he looked very smug when I saw him again. Only it made no difference. To make things worse, he announced that the cure would have to be repeated many times, both mine and hers. First he would come to anoint my member, and as soon as I was running screaming into a night illuminated spectacularly by that flaming torch planted in my groin, he would set to work on the woman.

Until one night I lost my temper where I sat beside the stream with my smoldering member buried in a huge mound of wet clay. Tears still streaming from my eyes, and steam billowing from my loins, I ran back to the village. The Moon was dead, but the reddish glow emitted by my firebird lit up the night, so that I came home rather sooner than the igqira must have expected me. I found him kneeling above my prostrate woman.

"Now don't you get the wrong thoughts, T'kama," he said in a voice choking with fear. "This is very special medicine I'm using on her. There is magic in this root."

I threw him out the door before he could say another word. This very nearly led to war, because he was the igqira and his people could not bear to see him insulted. But I told them I didn't care what magic he had in his root, the woman was mine. So every man picked up his assegai; and if old Khamab hadn't caught me by my glowing bird and dragged me off there would have been blood. Before the morning star was up we had to be gone, otherwise they would have slain us all, man, woman and child. They even set their dogs on us.* Some friends.

---

* *Would a black tribe at the end of the fifteenth century have kept dogs? It seems unlikely to me. Yet that is how I remember it.*

On a language lesson in the wilderness

In that year, if that was the year—

the year da Gama discovered the sea route around the Cape of Storms, six years before Hieronymus Bosch painted his "Last Judgment," the year when Leonardo turned forty-six and Michelangelo twenty-three, six years after Columbus had reached the coast of America and the Moors had been driven from Granada, thirteen years before Erasmus wrote *In Praise of Folly* and nineteen years before Luther's ninety-five theses, about three-quarters of a century after Mutota had founded the empire of Mwenemutapa (later more widely known as Monomotapa)

> in present-day Zimbabwe, and about one thousand two hundred years after the first people of the Christian era had settled in the Transvaal, thirteen years after Caxton had printed Malory's *Morte d'Arthur,* and forty-five years after the fall of Constantinople—

in that year our wandering through the wilderness began.

"It's all your fault," old Khamab was quick to tell me. "Why did you have to meddle with their igqira? Am I not good enough for you?"

"Nothing you did could help me with the woman, Khamab," I reminded him. "You know you've tried everything."

"Then it's time you realized it cannot go on like this. It's not just your life and the woman's, it's all of us." Or words to that effect.

"I'll go through the fire for her, Khamab."

"You've already gone through the fire, and look what happened."

"I won't ever stop trying."

"And what is to become of us?"

"We'll get through."

"Is this faith or pigheadedness?"

"Is there a difference?" I put my hand on his bony shoulder. "Just tell us which way to go so that we can get away from this place."

"You think we can ever escape the eye of Gaunab?" he asked angrily. But without waiting for an answer he turned his back on me and started fiddling with his medicine horn.

With deft fingers he maneuvered a strip of leather as thin as a blade of grass into his mixture of grease and herbs, then rubbed two sticks together to make fire and set the strip alight. As soon as it began to glow he cautiously held the horn against the wind to see which way the wisp of blue smoke would go. There was no need of explanation, we all knew the procedure. We set out in the direction the smoke had indicated. Day after day we proceeded like that, on a route that kept us roughly parallel with the coast.

Not that it helped much, for we seemed to carry the evil with us.

In the earliest times, when the first human beings were still fresh from Tsui-Goab's hands, those people had been much plagued by Gaunab, the Dark One, the Destroyer, who waged unending war against them. Tsui-Goab tried to protect his creatures. In the beginning he was beaten every time by Gaunab, but from every encounter he emerged stronger and stronger. Until there came a day—or a night, to be precise, because it was in utter darkness that Tsui-Goab lay sleeping beside a stream and Gaunab came upon him and the two began to wrestle—when he dealt Gaunab a death blow behind the ear. But as he fell, Gaunab struck out at him one last time and broke his knee. Which is where Tsui-Goab got his name, Lame-Knee.

And so the Dark One had been killed. But for us, if something dies, that does not mean it will be dead forever. Look at Heitsi-Eibib and his graves dotted throughout the wasteland of the interior: every time he came back to life. The same with Gaunab. And from harsh experience I can confirm this, for what was our interminable trek but a continuation of that first war between Gaunab and Tsui-Goab?

From the beginning the signs were there for all to see. That rare sight, stars streaking through the sky and dying in a rain of sparks, now occurring every night. *Hamerkop* birds perched at dusk in shallow water, treading the soft mud to stir up the spirits of the dead and foretell new deaths. A grasshopper chirping in the thatch of a hut. Whirlwinds chasing us in all directions, sometimes right into the trees. One day an old woman fell from such a tree, directly in the evil thing's way, and *sarês* whirled right over her, leaving her dead, every bone in her body broken. And all this to remind us that there was no getting away.

One night while we were singing our songs to T'kaam, the Moon, she was devoured by darkness right in front of our eyes, bite by bite, until there was nothing left but a dull rind.

And worst of all there was the woman stepping on a mantis in the grass one morning. She of all people. We couldn't even scream or groan, it was so bad. The people backed off in all directions and kept as far from her as possible. For that was a sure sign that she was carrying disaster with her.

"It's now or never," old Khamab warned me that night when we were alone together. "Tomorrow, when we move on, she stays behind. We cannot wittingly carry death with us."

And I must admit that for once I nearly succumbed. Yet something forced me to persist: "She didn't see the *t'gauab*. It was an accident. She doesn't even know why everybody is so upset."

"There is no need for her to know. And whether it was an accident or not is immaterial. It happened. That is enough. It is too much."

I shook my head, but what could I say? What she had done was an unequivocal sign that we were walking through a land of shadows. And the others were adamant. As we rose to set out the following morning there was no doubt at all in the gestures with which they motioned her to stay behind. They left with her a few calabashes of curdled milk, a bag of honey, an ostrich egg, as was the custom of our tribe when people too old or weak to travel had to be abandoned.

"You cannot do this," I whispered.

"Come on." That was all old Khamab said in reply. And from the way in which the men took hold of their kieries I could see that they were now past talking.

"Then I shall stay with her."

"Don't be stupid," said my friend Khusab. "You are our chu'que."

"I am not going without this one."

He hesitated, but old Khamab urged him on; and soon we could only see the dust of their trek against the early sun.

As I turned back I saw the woman staring at me, shielding her eyes with a hand. The naked fear in her face. But something else as well, which looked like pity.

"I'm staying," I said, but of course she couldn't understand.

It was not that she cried: but there were tears running down her face, tracing small furrows through the grease and buchu with which, like the other women, she had smeared herself; clutching the kaross tightly to her body, shrunken into a narrow bundle as if she would like to return to stone, growing back into the earth.

I came to her and pressed my finger to her forehead. "Khois," I said. And once again: "Khois."

Without any change in her expression, the tears still running down her face like rain, she took my hand in both of hers and repeated softly: "Khois. Woman."

I pressed my finger against my chest and said: "T'kama."

She found it difficult to shape the click with her tongue, but the word she said did bear some resemblance to my name: "T'kama."

Turning round I pointed to where the last dust was still lingering, and said: "Khoikhoin. People of people."

She lowered her head and I heard her saying: "T'kama." This time the click was very clear.

12

In which for the time being the narrative continues without the narrator

"Now you will have to lead us," old Khamab told Khusab as they descended toward a shallow ford in the first stream they reached, after half a day's walking. "With T'kama gone, we need a new chu'que."

"How can I take T'kama's place?" asked Khusab warily.

"That is how it should be."

"Suppose he comes after us?"

"He'll stay with the woman."

"This isn't a good thing at all, Khamab."

"It's T'kama who brought it on us. And there is only one way of getting Gaunab off our tracks."

But how could he, of all people, have expected Gaunab to give up so easily? It started at that very first ford through the stream: a stream so shallow it had been a mere trickle the last few times people had passed that way. That morning, too, it appeared harmless. And heavy-hearted as he was, Khusab began to cross with light feet, hardly looking where he stepped, there being almost no running water between the stepping-stones and slabs of cracked mud. But before he was halfway through there came a growling sound from the water below and it began to bubble as if it were at a boil. Screaming with fear, the people ran back helter-skelter to the bank, where they bundled together. Khusab hesitated for a moment, then began to sprint to the far side. Just in time he jumped clear, for by that time the water was up to his knees. The people were ready to scatter in all directions and that might well have been the end of the tribe if old Khamab hadn't managed, with much trouble, to calm them down, people and animals all in a scared huddle beyond the reach of the angry water.

It took him a long time to persuade them that the water had stopped growling and bubbling, having subsided once more to a quiet trickle among the flat rocks; and it stayed that way when the old man began to lead the people across in hesitant twos and threes. Only when, after a good while, Khusab deigned to come back gingerly from the opposite bank to lend a hand did the water suddenly start boiling and snarling again, and this time he very nearly did not reach the side. Old Khamab had to bury him in mud up to his waist to appease the burns on his legs. And the sun was already setting by the time the last people and sheep and cattle had finally been brought safely through the ford.

"I could have been dead today," Khusab said that evening after he'd got his voice back.

"Don't complain," said old Khamab. "You should be glad it was only your legs. If it had been T'kama, his whole future would have been scalded."

Neither he nor any of the others felt like discussing the event. There are things one should rather leave alone. But if old Khamab had thought that silence would help the tribe forget more quickly he was sadly mistaken. For day after day the misfortunes continued, and each time Khusab was involved.

The next thing that happened was to his wife, who at that time was expecting their second child. (The first was about thigh high, and people were beginning to wonder why the next one was taking so long, for Khusab was a strong man and his wife both hale and willing.) She was so healthy she could outrun a hare if she had to. But all of a sudden, one night, she was taken with the cramps and the child came out. Dead. She too nearly died, and she was left so weak that the people were forced to camp there for a whole week. That gave the jackals and night walkers time to discover the kraal of thorn branches, and soon there were losses among the sheep. What made it eerie was that, even though watchmen were put out at night, the sheep disappeared from right under their eyes without a bleat or a whimper.

"These are no ordinary jackals," old Khamab was finally

forced to admit. "Must be the *thas* jackal. Those are the dead coming back in the shape of animals to plague us."

When at long last Khusab's wife had recovered sufficiently for the trek to resume, they stuck to the foothills of a long mountain range where there was enough grazing. But then came the rocks. On a clear blue day, not a breath of wind, only a single koo bird writing its great silent curves in the sky as it watched the plains below, a number of heavy boulders came tumbling down from the tallest cliff above them, thundering down the slopes, tearing loose other rocks, sending sparks flying so that the whole mountain was heavy with the sulfur smell of lightning; and the people got such a scare they didn't know which way to run. The whole tribe might well have been wiped out, together with all their cattle and possessions, but as it turned out Khusab was the only victim. By rights he should have been dead, but at the last moment old Khamab grabbed hold of him and pulled him away, so only one of his legs was struck.

That night he suffered much pain, and old Khamab took him into his own hut to look after him. Which made things easier for the hyena. Got right into the shelter where Khusab's wife and child were sleeping, and dragged off the screaming boy. By the time the other people came running the hyena had disappeared into the night. If it was a hyena. Not even a marrow bone was left behind.

Anxious to move on, in spite of his wounded leg, Khusab urged his people to cover as much ground as possible the next day, after they had sprinkled fresh water over their encampment to discourage the night walkers and the Sobo khoin. Whether it was because of their great haste or because he had such trouble hobbling on one leg is difficult to tell, but late in the afternoon Khusab had his encounter with the snake. A cobra. Before he could properly take aim with his kierie the fangs had perforated the thick flesh of his calf.

Old Khamab immediately came running up with his knife, pushed Khusab to the ground, made a deep incision in his calf, and started sucking and spitting out the venom, sucking and spitting. Afterward he rubbed *gaib* from his horn into the cuts, powdered leaves and pounded roots, chameleon, bat, *tinktinkie,* shrew, covered with an ointment of grease and sweat and buchu from his own body. But Khusab continued to writhe with pain. Once more Khamab began to suck and spit, but all to no avail; and at the first light of day Khusab seemed to be on the verge of dying. As a terrible last resort, old Khamab ordered the most drastic remedy of all. A sheep was taken from the flock and skinned with great caution, taking care not to draw too much blood as the animal had to stay alive throughout the process, its bleating enough to cause the strongest man's legs to buckle. In spite of the almost human whimpering the knives continued relentlessly until the skin was stripped entirely from the animal. The whole tribe gathered to watch, knowing that if the sheep—reduced by now to a whitish, bluish bleating carcass—managed to get up and stagger off, there was hope: and scouring the veld in the direction the skinned animal had taken, one would be sure to find the cause of the evil. But if it refused to get up and remained where it was, it was all over for Khusab.

Only in this instance the naked sheep neither staggered off nor stayed. Struggling to its feet, it started turning round and round, like a person in a dagga stupor, or drunk with honey beer. Until at last it sank back to the ground, bleating pitifully, tears running from its eyes.

"What does this mean, Khamab?" the people asked.

"I don't know." It was the first time in his long life our old t'gai aob was forced to admit defeat. "I honestly don't know. He didn't walk and he didn't stay where he was either. My only advice is that we must turn back and fetch T'kama. We must keep on the move day and night without stopping to rest, until we have found our chu'que again."

"What about his woman?" asked Khusab, still groaning in agony.

"If he wants to keep her she must come. All I know is that Gaunab will destroy us all if we leave T'kama where we left him."

13

In which two birds prepare to die in the wilderness

That, at least, was how they afterward related the story of their aborted trek to me. While they were away I had been working on a shelter for the woman and me until we could decide what to do next. Like a weaver bird I built us a nest; like a weaver bird she kept on tearing it apart until it was completely to her liking. At night I kept a fire going to keep off the lions and other marauders of the dark, because they seemed determined not to leave us alone. During the daytime I was usually so tired from lack of sleep that I could barely stand on my two feet. And when one morning I lay down to rest in a spot of shade I fell into such a deep sleep that I was totally unaware of the woman's going off to forage for food. By that time there was nothing left of the small supply the tribe had given us.

If only she had first brought back the berries to ask for my advice, but I suppose she was so famished that when she came upon the shrub it never even occurred to her that they might be poisonous.

When I found her many hours later her stomach was emptying itself in both directions with such violence that she had almost lost consciousness. As I lifted up her head her eyes turned upside down. The berries in her vomit and her excrement—some chewed, others still whole—told me all I needed to know. Old Khamab would have known a remedy, I did not. I picked her up and carried her back to our nest. She was still groaning, but very faintly, and from the dead weight with which she lay in my arms I knew she was dying. I couldn't even speak to her: the words we had begun to exchange were too poor, too clumsy, for what I had to say. I wanted to tear out my guts like a wounded baboon. I wanted to scream like a thorn bush screaming at the sun. I wanted to bleed like an aloe bleeding in early winter. But there was nothing I could do. I couldn't even cry.

I stumbled into the bush in search of something I could not even name, scared to death at what I knew for sure I would find on my return. Yet I could not leave her there either. Even if it meant that I would have to watch over her body and keep away the vultures and the scavengers until it had decayed completely, returned to earth; or until I too was dead.

When I arrived back at our nest, Khamab and my people had returned.

In which the reader learns of the woman's incurable wound, as the tribe continues to wander ever more deeply into the valley of the shadow of death

Blue-bush roots and blue-bush twigs, mixed with powdered poison thorn and boiled in water, was what he gave her to drink, followed by a dose of *dassie* urine. Rubbed the still warm dung of goats into her stomach to ease the pain. Then added a good pinch of dried porcupine stomach to quench the fire in her insides. And the following day, when she was still deathly pale and trembling, he gave her regular doses of wild geraniums that had grown in red soil very far away. We stayed there until at last she was back on her feet; and all the while I kept her in the nest I had built for her, well away from the other people because the illness had made her t'nau. Only after she had completely recovered could the women wash her clean again, and then we all returned to where they had left Khusab for dead.

Except he wasn't dead at all. Sat waiting for us, all smiles, completely healed and strong again, with a calabash of honey at his side, and the carcass of a *duiker* strung up over the fire. A lion had brought it to him, he said. That sounded like Heitsi-Eibib's handiwork.

"Now all we need is for you to succeed with the woman," old Khamab told me. "Then the tribe can prosper again."

But succeed I didn't. No matter how wiry and thin I had become from all our wanderings and suffering, that bird in my loins continued to grow. For a while I kept it tied to my knee with a leather thong to keep it from swinging and slapping about; then to my calf, but still it went on growing, until I was getting worried it would get trampled underfoot or trip me up while walking. So I made a loop and tied the end to my waist with a *riem*. Bigger than the cobra that had attacked Khusab. And all for nothing; a useless, in fact obnoxious, appendage.

I remembered the story our old people used to tell about the first man on earth, the first *khoib* made by Tsui-Goab; and how he'd become so lonely that Tsui-Goab was forced to make him a wife, hewn from stone like himself. But because he had never seen a woman before, he had no idea of how to deal with her, so they simply lived together, side by side. Then, one day, he came upon a dry tree in the veld and decided to break branches from it for their fire; but the woman offered to climb it instead. And as she took up position above him, legs astride on two sturdy branches to start breaking firewood, he looked up and had the fright of his life. That gaping wound between her sloping thighs, which he had never noticed before. He took to his heels like a whirlwind across the plains, weeping and lamenting as he went. Until he nearly ran right off the edge of the world. But he was stopped just in time by Tsui-Goab, who asked him: "What is the matter?" And the man said: "A terrible thing has happened. My wife is dying. She is suffering from the most terrible wound you have ever seen." "Where is this wound?" asked Tsui-Goab. And the man said, "Between her thighs." Tsui-Goab clicked his tongue and said, "Tsk, tsk. Don't you understand, man? It is on account of that wound that I gave her to you and it is for the sake of that wound that you must care for her and love her."

Which was fine for him. But there I was with that woman at my side, the most beautiful woman Tsui-Goab had ever made, yet her wound had to remain untended because I was too big, and growing bigger every day. And if what old Khamab had said was true, that we would only prosper again once I had succeeded with her, that explains why our life, our trek, remained so hazardous. She had recovered from her illness, as had Khusab, but our struggles and sufferings continued unabated as we moved further and further, the mountains on our left and the sea far to the right, until we had passed the furthest places we had seen before.

From afar it had always seemed a fertile region, one green fold upon the other; but it turned out different. The streams were drying up; many days we trekked without a drop to drink. And because this was strange territory we could not, as on other journeys, rely on ostrich eggs and calabashes of water once buried there for future use. Neither were there *tsammas* in those parts. Only, few and far between, roots and acrid, fat-leaved shrubs; and sometimes we had to spread our karosses on the earth at night to catch the dew. But it was never plentiful, and animals and people were wasting thin.

As far as we went there were predators on our heels. No matter how many precautions we took, from one full moon to the next there would invariably be losses of sheep taken by leopards and hyenas and jackals. And they were getting bolder by the day as they grew used to our presence. In the middle of the day a leopard once dragged a small shepherd from his flock; his little comrades were ashen with fear when they came running with the news.

We had no choice but to organize a hunt. A whole day was set aside to ready our weapons, tuning and greasing the bowstrings, honing the arrowheads and dipping them in strong new poison. All the men set out together. It wasn't long before we found the spotted beast in a thicket. Khusab took aim. The arrow lodged deeply in the creature's shoulder, and with a roar it came storming from its hiding place, rolling and thrashing about trying to dislodge the arrow, then suddenly jumped up and made straight for us. A hailstorm of arrows, but he either dodged them or slapped them away. Not one stuck. One of the men went down under the leopard, his throat severed before we could move in for the kill. The beautifully marked skin we brought home with us, but no one was proud or cheerful, for it was a good man we had lost.

Soon afterward, as we sheltered in the mountains, we were set upon by a band of *Sonkwas*. Not a sound to warn us. Three of our men killed on the spot, at least half of the sheep driven off in the night, two young women dragged away. Once more we had to set out on a trek of many days and nights, without daring to call a halt, to get as far away as possible. But which way to go? Not even old Khamab knew the answer any longer. It became the kind of journey where one stayed on the move for the sake of moving.

And still I had the woman to worry about. By that time there were more and more words we could speak to each other, my Khoi words in exchange for those she had brought from far across the seas.* It was still not enough for us to sit down and have a proper conversation, but we had come a long way from mere silence, or from gesturing. Not that it was any help in what one might term our relationship. Every new attempt at entering her added alarmingly to the girth and length of my member. Soon I was able to wind it twice around my waist, like a hefty belt, the end tucked in. Which was reasonably comfortable, except when it got it into its obtuse head to stand up, because then it would break out of the loose knot I had tied and jump to attention, invariably hitting me like a lethal club between the eyes.

And still the misfortune continued. Children dying of illnesses no one had ever diagnosed and impervious to

---

* *Portuguese? For the life of me I can't remember.*

Khamab's medicine and magic. Twins born, to be exposed in the veld to appease the evil they represented. Predators. Sheep and cattle dying mysteriously. Drought. Hunger. Unbearable thirst. Inexplicable quarrels breaking out among the people. In one kierie fight two men were badly wounded, and afterward no one could explain what had caused it in the first place. Women flying into a rage and attacking each other with nails and teeth.

From time to time we would enter the territory of a black tribe, not yellow-brown like us; once or twice they were hostile, but most allowed us to stay. However, they were also suffering from the drought. They had known dry periods before, they told us, but never anything as severe as this. They had no food to share with us. In some places we were chased away like enemies because we threatened their meager food supplies; and they kept us away from their water. Which caused more sheep to die. On and on it went. And it got worse: for soon it was no longer a simple matter of animals and drought and sickness, but something terrifying and quite unheard of.

We first became aware of it when some of the children came home with stories of people they had met in the veld: people they had recognized. Recognized? Yes, indeed, they said excitedly, the people who had been killed in our great battle with the Beard Men on the beach. We scolded them for telling lies; when they came home the following day with the same kind of story we thrashed them until they could neither sit nor stand. But that same evening, beside our campfire, we saw those people with our own eyes: circling round and round us, keeping just beyond the edge of the light. I recognized them myself. And from then on Gaunab ran amok quite openly among us. Night walkers came into our temporary huts to suck the men dry and ride the women and terrify the children. Sobo khoin, Shadow People. The dun-colored ones. As if all the graves in that vast land had opened to vomit up their dead. Trees suddenly bursting into flames at night. Rocks breaking open to let out liquid fire. Snakes crossing our tracks and sprouting wings to fly off through the deadwood trees and disappear into the searing white light of the sun. Never before had we lived through times like those.

My only source of sweetness was the woman. We had begun to multiply our few words, to use them with new and different meanings, so that by now we could lie together at night and talk like people, whether in her strange language or in mine. We would share a handful of food. In the dark we would huddle together, even though it had to be back to back, or with her behind me, as my thing was too big for me to snuggle up against her: moreover, it would keep on twitching and jumping about so much that sometimes in my sleep it would drag me right out of the hut as if it had a terrible life of its own. And she with that incurable wound.

I was sorry for her. After all, it wasn't her fault. So why should she take my condition so much to heart? Or was there another reason? Yet for what other reason would she have begun to work so hard to make life bearable for me, whereas I should have been the one to care for her? She rubbed my bad shoulder. (Especially when it turned winter again the pain was sometimes very bad.) When there was something to eat she would share her portion with me. And now and then, when the desire became unbearable, she would try to comfort that intimidating bird-thing with her hands; then it would shoot up against the roof of the hut, where the jet would unfurl like a huge thistle, to rain its white wetness over us. But that was as far as we could go.

Perhaps it was the urge to be of use or help that drove her one day to kill a hare with a stone. We had all gone out into the veld in search of something—anything—to eat; and when we came back she was roasting the hare on the coals. I had never seen her look so proud. Licking a sliver of succulent flesh from a fragile bone she broke off a leg and held it out to me, calling happily:

"T'kama, come and eat."

We stood back in horror. She couldn't understand what was going on. It was, inevitably, old Khamab who finally grabbed a calabash of water to pour the precious liquid over her, and her fire, and the hare, while covering his eyes in the crook of an elbow.

"Woman!" he shouted, his reedy old man's voice breaking with shock and rage. "Do you really want to destroy us once and for all? Don't you know the hare is the messenger of death?"

When we came home from the veld the following afternoon the woman was gone.

15

Which features a failed attempt at copulation, with tragic consequences

By that time we had behind us a trek of many months through a large area of barren plains and brittle grass; but now we had entered a mountainous region where it was all too easy to get lost in great folds and knuckles and the dense virgin forest of deep kloofs. Impossible to follow a track for any distance. I was convinced that she'd got lost: gone, perhaps, in search of food, perhaps to atone in some way for the evil she had unwittingly brought upon us by killing the hare; and unable to find her way back through the undergrowth. More frightening possibilities—that the Shadow People had abducted her, or that Gaunab had changed himself into an eagle or a leopard to carry her away, knowing how mortally that would hurt me—I refused to consider. There were no traces of blood or struggle—not that this necessarily meant anything, as I knew only too well that Gaunab or the People from Beyond can come and go without leaving the slightest telltale sign.

In the little light remaining before sunrise the others reluctantly helped me to look for her, moving in ever wider circles around our camp. I knew I couldn't count on them for much; they were all angry about what the woman had done, even if they were cautious not to say too much in front of me; but at least they went with me until the dark came down.

"We shall look for her again at sunrise," I announced as we turned back.

Khamab glanced askance at me, hobbling along on his grasshopper legs. "It's useless, T'kama. She won't survive this night. It is too cold and she didn't even take a kaross with her. And then there are the animals."

I refused to answer, afraid I might crack up before him. But when I reached my hut there was a grasshopper chirping in the thatch; and in the night I heard an owl, which meant there were night walkers at large. What made it unbearable was the relief I perceived in the others. The way they saw it the evil that had dogged us from the start had finally skulked away.

Some of the people were eager to move on the following morning; and when I insisted we first resume the search, the thunderstorm that had been brooding among us for so long, like a lightning bird crouching in its anthill, suddenly broke loose.

"It's Tsui-Goab himself who took her away so that we can

have peace of mind again," they said. "We've been disobedient to him for long enough. Let the woman be, and let us go."

"We shall search for her first."

"Then let those who feel like it help you. The rest of us are going."

"You will do as I say, I am the chu'que."

"It is you yourself who have turned away from us."

They were clutching their kieries under their karosses. I could not face another fight among ourselves. So with a sigh I turned away. "Go then. But this thing will bring sorrow to you all."

It seemed to be moving toward a peaceful resolution. But when they began to round up some of the cattle and sheep to drive off with them, I intervened: "If you want to go, then go. But the animals belong to the tribe."

"We're part of the tribe."

"The tribe is where I am."

"Then try to stop us."

And so it happened that for the first time in our history a full-scale war broke out among ourselves; and all for nothing, owing to an act of treachery: while the battle was still raging, the deserters surreptitiously sent some of the children to open the kraal and turn out the sheep. Before this led to even more senseless carnage we had to give up and let the traitors go. Worst of all was the suspicion that even some of those who remained with me were not wholly loyal anymore. Some of them had been shaken by the needless violence.

As I look back now, the whole incident becomes even more pointless because the search for the woman turned out to be fruitless after all.

For most of the time, as we continued through the following days to scour the plains and mountains for her, we kept close together; but sometimes I set out on my own, even if it was against Khamab's wishes. By that time I was so short-tempered that even he felt reluctant to object openly: only once, when yet another group deserted us in the night, he cautiously asked me whether I didn't think it had gone far enough. I did not answer. What could I say?

Wandering about on my own like that one day I came upon two tortoises on a steep incline. Heaven knows what had so desperately fired their mating urge in the very heart of winter; they must have been desperate. A tortoise male will travel for days to find a female. When I arrived he had just found her. He tried to corner her this way and that, but every time she got away. Amazing how fast a female tortoise can move when she's made up her mind. But with dour determination he went on, and in the end he managed to steer her among some fallen rocks where there was no way out for her. There he mounted her, a laborious process, his front legs rowing in the air like stubby, scaly wings vainly trying to fly, his neck stretched out so far it seemed he was going to climb right out of his shell, while he tried to bend his hard back so that he could get in under her recalcitrant carapace. And just as his beady black eyes began to bear an expression suggesting he was almost there she suddenly rose up under him, steadying her crooked front legs on a flat stone, and threw him off so that he landed right on his back, clawing in futile panic at the empty air. But she had also miscalculated the maneuver, and as she swung round to scuttle past him two of her legs slipped under her so that she, too, fell over.

There they would both have died. But knowing what frustration meant I took pity on them, and carried them back to our encampment, where I cut off their heads; and that evening at least we had tortoise soup to eat, sweet, soft meat to make life livable again. The curious thing about the whole experience was this: after we had finished all the soup, what remained at the bottom of the pot were not two shells as one might have expected, but two large round stones.

16

Concerning a conversation on the edge of the abyss

When I found her—time had stopped by then; it was a day outside all calculation—at first I could not believe my eyes. She must have died long ago; it must be, I thought, a spirit, or some trick Gaunab was playing on me. Because I had been walking all day, very cautiously, on the trail of a lion. The previous night the great beast had come right up to our huts, growling so loudly that the earth had trembled; and that had made me think that if I could track him down, and supposing he made a kill and then left the carcass, having had his fill, I might eventually fight off the vultures and the scavengers for a piece of meat. But then it was not the lion I found, but her, perched high on a rock, on a tall pinnacle stained red and yellow with centuries of sun and rain and dassie urine and lichen: and beyond her the earth seemed to fall away into an abyss whose like I'd never seen before. From a distance it seemed as if we had reached the very end of the world. Only when I edged up more closely, cautiously, like a leopard stalking his prey, did I notice an end to the tumbling cliffs below her: far, far below the earth continued, an expanse of trees and shrubs so dense it seemed like a sea of green, fading into a gray distance where it was impossible any longer to distinguish sky and earth.

"Khois."

She did not even turn her head, merely pulled in her shoulders as if preparing to jump.

"How did you get here?" I asked.

I could not walk the last few yards to her, she was too far away.

"I thought you were dead."

Only then did she look round, as if she found my presence as unbelievable as I did hers.

I was unable to steer my conversation in any direction; whatever I could think of seemed confused and superfluous. All I really wanted to say, over and over, was "Khois. Khois. Khois."

She shrugged vaguely.

"There was a lion following you. You didn't even notice."

"I know all about him."

"You do?" I gaped.

"Yes. He looked after me."

"Now I know you are dead. No live person would talk like that."

(Could it have been Khusab's lion? I thought much later.* But surely that was preposterous. That had been seasons and landscapes ago. And lions simply do not do that kind of thing.)

It was the woman who first spoke again, after we had both been silent for very long. "Why have you come?" It sounded like an accusation.

"Why?! How can you ask that? I haven't stopped looking for you since the moment you disappeared." I stared at her. She didn't turn her eyes away. "Khois, what has happened? Did you lose your way? Did something"—for the first time I dared to say it; she was safe—"did something carry you off?"

She frowned, and seemed perplexed by my question. "I ran away," she answered simply.

I couldn't believe it. "Just like that? You ran away?"

"My God," she said softly. "Don't you understand? I couldn't bear it any longer. I can't do anything right. I understand nothing about you or your people or this goddamned country. There's nowhere I can go to. My own people abandoned me long ago. Everything is impossible. I have nothing left, no possessions, no future, no hope, no faith, not even clothes. What am I doing here?"

Behind her: the earth falling away into the abyss.

"Neither of us can run away, Khois. We can only go on."

"Where to? There *must* be an end to it somewhere."

---

* *See Chapter 14 above.*

"There is no end if we are together."

"I wanted to die," she said. "Why couldn't I die? I tried. I thought I'd starve myself to death, it should be so easy, but then the lion brought me food. I wanted it to kill me, but it wouldn't. Then I thought I'd freeze to death, but at night it came to lie beside me and kept me warm. I tried to jump from this cliff, but again the lion stopped me. Please, won't *you* kill me, T'kama?"

"I've come for you. You must live with me."

"I thought: If only I could get away. So far that nothing and no one will ever find me again, not even I."

"And now?" I asked it so quietly I could barely hear my own voice.

She looked at me. "Now I'm exhausted. That's all."

"What do you want to do?"

"I don't know. I know nothing anymore." Her face quiet with pain, dark as the sea. "I don't want to run away anymore. But I don't know what I *do* want. All I know is that I don't ever again want to be where you are not."

I went to her. In total silence we sat together in the light of that transparent day. And that is how I still see us in my memories: man and woman in the beginning of the world, a desperate world. Beside each other, but without touching. Not a hand that moves, no wind, not even a breath or hint of it, only the words. I am thinking words. I remember another day when I was standing thinking words, but then, in a way, it was still easy. What I think now is: love. I think: fear. I think: revolt, despair. And I think: all of this is but a voice, sounds shaped by a throat and a mouth and disappearing into silence. Why these sounds and not others?

Surely I might just as well have thought: Lambs. Us. Oltnka. Hangtree. Grstlm. Behind each separate sound opens a chasm, an abyss. New worlds beginning. Without end. And, like her, I know nothing else anymore. Except the words. I think: I am afraid. I am alive. I love.

17

On word and flesh, and on how once again a woman is left in the lurch

Love, indeed. But what could be *done* about it? One does not live only through words, but through flesh as well. And I was so excessively endowed with it. Merely seeing the woman again led to a mighty resurrection of the flesh. As for willingness, I had more than enough of it. And I daresay the woman too. But how to cleave her cleft with that enormous tree of mine? The very efforts I made to enter her caused it to grow to such a size that I was staggering on my feet to keep my balance. Yet there was nothing, absolutely nothing I could do about it. And after the thing had finally subsided—there were moments when I feared it would never do so again—I had to wrap it round my waist in four or five large loops, and tuck the angry head in under them, for fear of becoming the cause of stumbling to others. Would my fate have been easier to bear had I known in advance what I know now and what will be revealed to the reader in the crocodile episode of the next chapter?* Or worse? It is pointless to speculate. All I know is how unbearable it seemed right then. Everything lies embedded in the weight of this word. And throughout that long first night I lay with her after finding her again, she lying fruitless and awake beside me, I was thinking heavily: If this bird keeps on growing like this, Khois and I will need no kaross next winter; we will be able to wind it warmly around us both. In due course it will be easier to go around her than to come inside her.

---

* *The reader is requested not to turn the page before the time: in a story everything has its appointed place.*

18

Concerning an adventure that, had it not been real, might easily have been a dream; or vice versa

At dawn we returned to the handful of people who had loyally remained with me, and together we resumed our journey: that was the turning point for us. In a wide curve we began to move south again. Hope springs eternal. But instead of improving, however impossible it seemed, conditions actually grew worse.

It was a landscape designed by the sun: pure light and rock. For days on end we trekked without encountering bird or animal or even a shadow. The withered wooden skeletons of trees that had grown there long ago were scattered in fantastic shapes in the heat, cracked open and pulverized by the violence of the sun, the roots frayed like charred intestines. A few remaining brittle blades of white grass stood trembling in what wind there was, offering not a mouthful of food to the emaciated sheep. There was no living, growing thing to be seen anymore: in that terrifying landscape not even the stones could grow.

Exhausting all the ceremonies he knew, old Khamab desperately tried to make the rain come down, but the sky was like a cow that had lost her calf and balked at being milked. He sent us into the veld in search of rare chameleons. If we found one, it was buried gently, upside down, care being taken not to harm it in any way. In the past this remedy had invariably brought rain within the very day: but not this time. When that didn't work, we tried a cobra. Still nothing. After that we buried round stones in the sand. Nothing. Two children born years ago in a rainstorm were sent out one by one ahead of us to attract the rain, but the first was bitten by a snake and the second simply vanished, his tracks stopping in the middle of a patch of sand. Enough to make one feel cold in the middle of the day. And still there was no sign of rain.

On full-moon nights, exhausted and weak as we were of hunger and exertion and thirst, we danced from sunset to sunrise, singing our rain songs:

"Full Moon, Oh Moon,
We welcome you, Moon,
Welcome, Tsui-Goab,
Give us honey,
Give our cattle grazing,
So that they can give us milk."

In a large circle the men sat blowing on their *ati,* rattling the t'koi-t'koi, tugging at the string of the gurah, while the women clapped their hands and danced around us. Perhaps we were still being punished for the hare we had killed, the doomed messenger of the Moon; perhaps it was because of the woman, perhaps there was another cause: whatever it was, in that unholy land no rain ever fell.

All game had migrated long ago, so we had nothing to fear from predators. But what difference did that make? Death traveled with us all the way. And of other kinds of danger we had to contend with I hesitate to write today, for who would take my word for it? Who would believe that great boulders came into our shelters at night and devoured our children? That hardwood tree trunks attacked our men and knocked them down when they scavenged for food in the moonlight? That the storm wind violated our women and caused their bellies to swell, but without children, mere airbags that brought nothing but pain?

That was how it went. And in a way I suffered even more than the others, because in addition to our common afflictions I had that mighty bird to contend with day and night as it weighed me down and dragged me this way and that and wrenched me to my knees and sapped my strength. The woman was too scared to come near me, for when it reared up and went into a gallop it smashed everything within reach, so that most mornings the hut looked like a place hit by an earthquake. My own people were beginning to avoid me. A real quandary it was: without me they could not go on; with me they wouldn't.

I often thought of Heitsi-Eibib's history: of how his

mother had eaten grass and was impregnated by the green sap, how she gave birth to a son who slept with her to engender more sons and brothers; and how he died many deaths, only to rise again after each burial. But for the woman with me there was no grass. She had nothing at all. And she suffered.

It was in that time, on the most barren and arid plains we had ever reached in our wanderings, that we came upon the river. On the long trek there we had often seen visions of water: pools and lakes and streams, green *vleis* surrounded by reeds and rushes and dancing plumes, once even a turbulent green sea. But every time it disappeared before we could reach it, often after many days of feverish travel during which we'd had to leave behind us people and sheep and possessions so that we could move faster. But this river did not vanish. When we first saw it in the distance, we began to run toward it, then slowed down to a walk; in the end we were crawling on all fours, stalking it cautiously so that it would not disappear like the others. But it stayed in place, and we reached it, a wide, shiny snake with greenish edges slithering across the rocks. It came from nowhere, breaking straight out of the parched earth a few hundred yards upstream to surge between its banks; and half a day's journey lower down—we discovered afterward—it dove underground again to continue on its invisible course, with not a sign on the surface to betray its deep presence. A weird sight to behold. But it was water, it was a miracle, and it was there.

After the first incredulous pause to make quite sure it was real, people and animals broke into a stampede down the steep bank, where we hurled ourselves headlong into the water. We drank and drank until our bellies were like calabashes, and then some more; some remained on all fours, unwilling or perhaps unable to stand up. It was a long time before they came to their senses again. It was at that stage that the shout rang out:

"Crocodile!"

Who could believe it? In that stretch of placid water? But it was true, as true as the river itself.

If the charge into the stream had been something to behold, the flight from it was even more spectacular. To an outsider watching from a distance it might even have been hilarious, but not right there in the midst of the screaming, splashing horde.

I was also on my way out—chasing most of the others before me, as their safety was my responsibility—when there was a new shout from those who had already reached the top of the tall bank: "There, there!"

They were pointing at something in midstream.

In the middle of the river, where it was at its deepest, too deep for standing, I saw the white woman thrashing about. There was not one among us who could swim, it was not in our nature; but she must have been so overjoyed by the water that she was carried far beyond our reach.

"Hurry!" I shouted at her. "It's right behind you!"

With flailing arms and legs she was coming closer to the side, but the crocodile was much faster.

That was when I discovered that no matter what Tsui-Goab chooses to allow, nothing is ever in vain.

In retrospect I remember the whole episode the way one

remembers a dream. But even standing on that spot that day, staring at what was happening in front of my eyes, it felt like a dream. Now the way of a dream is this, whether it be wet or dry, a dream of love or of war, frightening or joyous: it causes a man to rise up. I felt the thing withdraw its head from the lasso around my waist, and unwind itself, whirring round and round my body at dizzying speed: it was like a thong suspended from a crossbar to be cured, a stone tied to the bottom so one can wind it up tightly and let go. There was the swooshing sound of a whirlwind all around me as it unfurled itself to rear up in a straight hardwood pole that stretched halfway across that wide river.

"Grab it!" I shouted at the woman.

And she grabbed. And she began to pull herself to shore, hand over hand. In a white foam of churning water the crocodile came after her. Faster and faster she came toward me, until at last she was close enough for me to seize her by the arms. I bent over, and reached forward, and caught hold of her, and hurled her up against the bank. Then, stumbling, I tried to turn round to follow her. But with that tremendous trunk staggering from the fork of my body I lost my balance, stepped into a mudhole, and toppled over. Like an impossible water snake my member came after: but at that moment the crocodile lurched forward and slammed its jaws shut with a sound of great rocks clashing. In front of my eyes I saw the river turn to red. I heard the crocodile thrashing the water with its tail. At that stage I felt no pain. But I did not need pain to tell to me what I already knew: my bird had been snapped right off.

19

In which is demonstrated the relative nature of gain and loss

It was the last thing old Khamab did in his life, for by that time he was older than old, and the long trek had exhausted him: but he still had enough strength left to tend me in the hut my people had hurriedly set up for me: a framework of dry branches, covered with skins. There was late daylight outside: inside a dense round darkness, like the darkness I imagine inside a woman. When I regained my consciousness in that womblike night I thought I must be dead. Surely no man could survive a catastrophe like that: I had lost the greater part of my body.

But then I heard the old man scurrying beside me, uttering brief groans of exertion or content.

"What are you doing, Khamab?"

"Keep still, else it will start bleeding again. I've never in my life seen bleeding like this. The whole river was red."

I couldn't stop myself from moving one hand to feel the wound. There was nothing to feel. It was like a woman. Blunt. Not even a stump. Only the balls were, surprisingly, intact.

"You should have let me die, Khamab."

"Lie still."

"What are you doing?"

"How does this feel?" He put something in my hand. "Be careful, the clay is still wet."

My eyes had become used to the dark by now, and I could see what he had made: a new male-bird fashioned from clay. After what I had grown used to this little instrument seemed puny.

"What shall I do with a thing like this?"

"More than with your old one." He clicked his tongue impatiently. "Well, what do you think? It's not every man has the chance of choosing his future."

I turned away my head. "Make it any way you want to, I don't care. What use is a thing made of clay?"

Grunting, he went on working. Without meaning to, I turned to have another look. He was working with the dedication of a boy making a clay ox; his mouth half-open. I could hear him breathing heavily, unevenly. The old man was finished. With lashings of spittle he softened the clay to add something here, take away something there, roll the body out more thinly, evenly, rounding the head, testing it in the palm of his hand to check the weight and shape.

When at long last he was satisfied, he struggled wearily to his feet and called through the doorway. The woman came inside. Outside, the night was coming down like a dark kaross. I could hear the people making fire.

"What do you need the woman for?" I asked. The numbness was draining away; I was beginning to feel pain.

Old Khamab paid no attention to me. "Lie down," he told the woman.

Did she protest? I don't remember. Perhaps by that time she was so resigned that she no longer cared.

He tested his handiwork on her. Meticulously, each time making a few small adjustments. His breath was very shallow by now. I had heard people dying before; I knew he was coming close.

Because of the state of semiconsciousness I was in, I find it difficult clearly to recall what happened. But after a long time he joined the thing—smooth and wet from the woman's insides—to my body. Using spittle, mainly, I think. But also thorn-tree gum, and beeswax, and ancient herbs, and goat fat, and stinking and fragrant medicines from that horn of his, inexhaustible even after our long, dry trek.

"It's useless, Khamab," I groaned.

With great difficulty he bent over me and began to blow his warm, unsteady breath over my loins. I could not believe it. Slowly, slowly, like a wind dying down, the pain went away.

Then he stopped, panting like a man who has run too far.

"What's the matter, Khamab?"

He sighed. "Nothing. I am weary. This was too much for me, I think."

How well I remember his face the way I saw it then, for the last time, cracked and worn like a dried-up vlei. I could not have thought it then, but I think it now: that his face was like an old map, showing all the places he had been to. (And what would—will—my own face reveal of this dry land one day?)

For the last time he turned the muddy moisture of his old eyes in my direction before he began to crawl on all fours toward the door. There he glanced back at the woman and said: "Now it's up to you."

She sat quietly in the dark for a long time as if she were suddenly shy to face me. And scared. As scared, no doubt, as I was.

I didn't know why I said it, but at last I said: "Khois? Help me."

When she laid her hand on me I could feel the clay creature warming up, stirring, swelling slowly, as if coming alive, turning to flesh.

"Khamab?" I called. He did not answer. I raised myself on my elbows, but the old man was no longer in the doorway where he'd been.

From outside, for a while, I could hear the night sounds of my people. But then the sounds died down and it became very quiet: not the silence of absence, but a silence suggesting a terrifying intensity of life. As if once again all of them, man, woman, and child, were drawn in a tight circle around the hut to listen to what was happening inside.

I wanted to call the old man back. I needed him. I was terrified. But in the dark—I couldn't really see her, could only feel her body close to mine—the woman placed a finger on my mouth; I could feel her shaking her head. Her long hair on my shoulders.

"There're only the two of us, T'kama. It's up to us."

I knew how easy it was to fail. I knew how dangerous it was to be alive.

From outside I become conscious of another sound: even and rustling, softly at first, then more and more insistently, the sound of *sibi*.

It was raining.

She was right: there were only the two of us now; it was up to us.

20

*A short chapter that may be skipped by readers who object to descriptions of sexual intercourse**

The rain that rained: every crack and crevice in the parched earth overflowed with wetness, and from deep tunnels emerged snakes and meerkats. Where there had been only death, new life broke out, dry beds of marshes were squelched with moisture, every hollow filled up heavily with water. High above, the clouds were on fire with lightning, forking and branching down to earth. Even hills and mountains seemed to swell with life, nudging each other like lustful men and women; tearing themselves loose

---

* *Which prompts the question whether such a reader shouldn't skip the whole book.*

from the earth, the trees began to dance; all the world was translated into song, one huge voice exulting to the sky: pure voice, all voice, nothing but voice, a scream that broke the mountains and split the earth: rocks voice, trees voice, animals voice, human beings voice, all things returned to voice, the first language of all language, sound, hallelujah. A flood washing away all that had been, cleansing utterly what remained, glistening with wetness and birth, until a new sun broke through to bellow over all that lives: *I am!*

21

In which a circle is completed

Back to where we started. From a last high hill—harsh green grass billowing in the wind, lower down dense thickets in the kloofs, blue flowers, yellow patches, aloes, thick-fingered euphorbias—we can see the wide sweep of the bay, where blue waves dissolve in foam. With a sudden fear in the pit of one's stomach one glances at the horizon, but there is nothing. The sea is virginal.

Beside me, the woman; and our child who has already learned to run short distances. She is still suckling him, refusing to wean him, possessive, jealous, angry, beautiful. Because of the milk in her breasts she has not yet begun to swell with another child, but that will come.

Back at our old encampment we repeat the ritual of immemorial times: from the river, where it debouches into the sea, we collect clean mud to plaster on our foreheads, with soot from the first fire kindled on the ashes of the old. On the decayed graves of the people we left behind we sprinkle fresh water. One must make friends with the water of a place before you can settle in it again. High on the hill Heitsi-Eibib's cairn has been plundered by the wind, the cross dismembered; it must be repaired. Only then dare we gather fresh branches to build our huts anew.

There is a long journey behind us. But the land has been generous and kind ever since the day I first entered the woman, the night old Khamab died. The rains continued. Throughout the Karoo the veld was bountiful. Sheep bush. Sweet grass. Thorn trees yellow with flower puffs. What had remained of our sheep and cattle flourished and multiplied again.

Now, after all this time, we can come to rest again.

But how curious that there should have been this restlessness among the tribe. As if all were secretly waiting for something to happen. No one dared to mention it, but it was there. It bothered me. I knew only too well what it was: I could see it in the intentness of the stare with which, when she didn't know I was watching her, the woman peered at the sea. A stare so fixed and furious it seemed her eyes would pry something from the blue, something that did not yet exist but that she wanted to make happen.

And then, suddenly one day, five ships came drifting from that blue expanse—coming close enough for us to make out, at the beak of the one in front, the torso of a naked woman—no one was really surprised. From the beginning we had known that it was only a matter of time. They were not the same ships as before, of course not, we could all see that at a glance; but what difference did that make? There had been intruders before them; now they were there; others would come after them. Our shore was exposed and open, like a woman already taken. The way it had been it could never be again.

Having warned my people to keep out of sight, I went up the rocky hillside to the cairn to watch from there. At a hollow below the slope I stopped for a while. Then squatted down, digging aimlessly among the old bones bleached by the sun, worn thin by the wind. So many, many bones, one might dig up the whole hill and not come to the end of them. People and people and people, reaching further back than Heitsi-Eibib himself. All those who had been there before us. It occurred to me that, in fact, the whole land might be made of bones, but thinly covered by a layer of soil and rock and trees and shrubs. Was there ever an end to it?

I resumed my climb to the top.

From the ships came rowing boats, exactly as the previous time. I could see how excited the Beard Men became when they discovered our footprints on the sand. They spread out on the beach and ventured to the edge of the bush, where they stopped to shout at the land, hands opened against their mouths to amplify the sound. Then turned their heads sideways, listening, as if expecting a reply. But my people kept quiet.

Except I knew it would not go on like that. The strangers had seen our tracks, and they would continue to explore until they'd found something.

"Let us go hunting," I ordered my men the following day.

"We must avoid trouble this time. Perhaps, if we offer them a buck, they'll see that we mean well. Then they may leave us in peace."

But when we returned in the late afternoon there was pandemonium at our place. It took much angry shouting before the women would tell us what had happened: it seems that some of the children had stolen away to spy on the strangers; discovering it, the women had followed in haste. Exactly what had then happened on the beach no one could tell for sure. To me, only one thing mattered: that the woman, my woman, Khois, my white woman, the smooth beautiful one, the one with the long dark hair, with the round breasts, that she had gone back with the Beard Men to the nearest boat.

22

In which the male protagonist tries to understand the woman's point of view before returning (characteristically) to a preoccupation with himself

Should I have taken heed before? Had I really concerned myself enough with my woman's reactions to the return of the ships? The very fact that, afterward, it took such effort to recall the expression with which she had stared at them, accuses me. And only when it was too late did I sit down to try to remember: as I am trying now, centuries later, and with even less hope of success, to reconstruct what she might have thought and felt.

There was a pool of silence deep inside her, yes, that I do

remember. All she did was stand there, staring. But staring with an intensity shaped in the very marrow, as if she had to dislodge a whole life—past, present, future, everything—from the little her eyes could see.

Would she have been thinking: My God, they're back, at last, now I can go home?

Or: No, please, don't let this happen, not after I have finally found a home here, a husband, and a child?

I came from behind. My shadow fell on her. She seemed to tremble lightly, even before I could put my arm around her, cupping my hand on her breast. She said nothing, but I could feel the stiffness in her body, resisting me; resisting most of all, perhaps, herself.

"Khois: what are you looking at?"

"Nothing."

"What do you think those strangers have come for?"

"How must I know?" Angrily, as if she resented my having asked.

"Are you scared, Khois?"

"Why should I be scared?"

"*I* am scared."

She turned round swiftly, pressing her head against my shoulder. "Hold me tight," she said, so quickly I could barely make out the words. "Just hold me."

She was trembling. For a long time we didn't speak. At last she seemed to relax. She looked up at me, almost expressionless, her face as calm as the sea.

"Come," I said.

"Where to?"

"Back to our place."

For a moment she yielded, then held back. "You go. I'll come later."

"There's nothing to stay for here. Come."

"Just let me be!" Such anger in her, it scared me.

"Why won't you tell me what is troubling you?"

"There *is* nothing to say. Don't you understand?"

Through her words I saw the emptiness behind them. I wanted to take her in my arms again, but she wouldn't. I turned around and went home alone. The child had to be looked after. Only once did I look back: she was still standing there, motionless, her face to the sea. Far on the horizon the small ships lay, rocking gently on the easy swell.

I know now I should have turned back. Just to be with her. We could dispense with words. Perhaps, if I had gone back, in some mysterious way, who knows, something would have been communicated to her, from my body to hers, blood to blood and bone. And then she would have known. *I* would have known. But I was offended by her aloofness. I thought: If she refuses to speak, then I'll wait until she decides to say something. I won't force her.

Which is why I still don't know. That is all I know. That I do not know.

And I thought I knew her.

Inside me: an abyss of fear and pain, incurable pain. Because there is nothing so terrifying as to lose the one you love without knowing where to look for guilt or reasons. Even without being able to say: Remember me, remember me, remember me.

23

Offering another view of the woman's departure

"Let her be," said the old man K'guda who had taken Khamab's place as our medicine man. "She's back where she belongs. We don't want to see those troubles starting all over again. It's good riddance."

24

In which the story of the betrayal of Adamastor by Thetis is told once again, but really for the first time

"She did not go willingly, T'kama," one of the old women told me, in great confidence, while I was trying to feed the child milk from a calabash. "The others were too scared to tell you. They still feel uneasy about your white woman with the smooth hair. But I shall tell you everything. She tried to run away with us, but she stumbled and fell, and the strangers caught her. I could see her kicking and struggling, and we could hear her screaming for a long time still, but they took her away."

In a profound way it made me feel relieved. The anguish that had settled in my stomach like a lump of cold porridge that would not digest began to dissolve. Only afterward did the questions return: Suppose the old woman had lied just to comfort me? How can one ever be sure about lying or telling the truth? Still, I believed her. I *wanted* to believe her. Her words had made sense. One doesn't just take a woman and go off with her as I had done: there are ways of acting that must be respected. Parents and elders to be consulted and appeased. A bride price to be paid. That was the way it had always been. That was the way I would have acted had the k'onkwa allowed me to obey our customs right from the beginning: but then the war erupted, the *torob* that destroyed it all. Now, at last, it seemed the time was ripe for me to make amends. I would go to the Beard Men and talk with them: this time, at least, it would be possible to talk, as through the woman I had learned some of their language. At least we would be able to understand each other.

I put the child to sleep and went to old K'guda to discuss what was to be done. He was reluctant at first, as you will know from the previous chapter, but in the end he agreed. As long as the negotiations were peaceful, he was prepared to support me.

In the dark predawn I set out toward the beach, accompanied by K'guda and three of the others—I did not want too many with me, lest the Beard Men misunderstand our intentions—taking with us two cattle and five sheep. On the ships everything was still quiet, nothing moved. We took up position where we would be clearly visible, squatting down patiently to wait. And at high day they acted as we had hoped they would: from the distant ships rowing boats were let down and began to move in our direction, the oars moving impressively in unison.

The strangers were cautious, however. They were holding their guns in readiness. But we waited without flinching, our hands held out toward them so they could see we were unarmed; and at length, moving slowly, step by step across the naked beach, they came right up to us and started making elaborate gestures toward the sea.

"There is no need for signs," I told them in the words the woman had taught me. "I can speak your language."

Immediately there was a change of attitude. And for the first time K'guda and the others with me began to relax.

"We brought you these oxen and sheep as tawete."

Without more ado some of the Beard Men hurried back to their boat and returned with armfuls of copper and beads and other precious things. And rolls of tobacco. And a small keg of brandy. This time I was careful not to offend them by refusing anything.

After we had all smoked and drunk together and shaken hands and sworn friendship I cautiously broached the reason for our coming. I was in debt to them, I said. What on earth could I be owing them? they asked. A bride price, I said. For the woman I had taken from their predecessors and whose price I was eager to pay according to our custom and undoubtedly theirs.

All at once they closed up in suspicion, one could see it in their eyes.

After a silence, the one who spoke for them said: "It is a matter we must first discuss among ourselves."

"By all means. Talk it over and decide on your price. I shall pay what you ask."

They returned to the boats, where they remained for a

very long time. We could see them waving their arms and talking earnestly. At last they came back with an answer. Five head of cattle and twenty sheep.

But when we arrived late that afternoon to deliver the bride price there was no sign of the woman among them.

"We shall bring her in the morning," the Beard Men promised. "She needs a full night's sleep so that she can be properly prepared."

I could not shut an eye all night. But when the boats came out to the beach the following morning there still was no sign of Khois.

"We have discussed it with our leader," their spokesman explained—they seemed nervous, clutching the guns as he spoke, which made me suspicious—"and he says the price we fixed on his behalf was too low."

"Then tell us what more you want."

"What are you prepared to pay for the woman?"

"Whatever you say."

"Bring us ten more oxen and twenty sheep this afternoon."

But when we came back there was still no sign of the woman.

"What is the matter now?" I asked, watching them drive the lowing, bleating flock into the boats; rocking wildly, those flimsy shells appeared too small for all of them.

"Come to the beach tonight and you will have her. There must be no one else with you. We shall bring you the woman. But you must wait patiently until the full moon has fully risen." He pointed to the sky overhead.

What else could I have done? I ordered my people to

keep away from the beach and in my absence to follow our ancient custom of paying homage to T'kaam; nothing should be neglected, and if all went well there would be even greater cause for celebration before the Moon was down.

I went down to the white beach, all alone, and waited in the shadows of the bushes until the Moon was high before I walked out on the cool fine sand. The dark sea was moving and tossing in the night, the breaking waves flecked with white as if broken shards of the Moon were shining from right inside them. I looked around. There was no sign of life. I felt my insides contract with anxiety. But I admonished myself: perhaps it was still too early. All I could do, had to do, was wait. She would be coming soon. Hadn't we agreed on that? Hadn't they promised? We understood each other; we were friends.

After a very long time, when the Moon began to slant, and as I began to walk along the beach, I suddenly noticed the dark figure between me and the dazzling path of the Moon on the water. Motionless, tall, pale, with long hair: the woman. For a moment I was petrified. She was standing so still I was sure it must be a ghost, one of the Shadow People, a moon mirage. But then, beside myself, my voice broke from my throat and I started running toward her. It *was* the woman. It had to be. Who else could it be?

"Khois! Khois! Khois!"

At full speed I ran into the heavy figurehead. For that was what it was. The figurehead from their main ship, which they had planted in the sand for me. Half dazed, I fell down in the shallow foam. And suddenly there were voices around me, and a horde of men came running from behind the rocks, where they had hidden, grabbing me, pulling me this way and that, kicking and beating me, until at last they began to drag me across the dark sand and up the high hill to Heitsi-Eibib's cairn, where they tied me to something, while I saw my own voice fluttering from my mouth like a wounded owl.

It was a great boulder to which they had lashed me with their seaman's ropes, my arms and legs stretched out, the knots so tight I could not move, no matter how fiercely I pulled and struggled. And then they fell on me, attacking every exposed and vulnerable part of my body—what had been mine from the beginning and what old Khamab had added to me.

"That will teach you to consort with our white women!"

It was a long, turbulent time before they left. The beach became deadly quiet, deserted as it must have been in the beginning of time. There was only me.

Through the blood I saw the sun come up, a great eye slaughtered on the horizon. In the farthest distance—but perhaps it was my imagination—the great seabirds were sailing off proudly and beautifully to wherever they had come from.

There was a terrible urge in me to shout: "Khois!" But my voice was like a fistful of old feathers thrust into my throat.

A black shadow came swooping down from high above. A vulture. Then another, and several more. Among the rocks, among the tall stones scattered from Heitsi-Eibib's cairn, they perched, stretching their bare necks to peer at me. Eat my heart, I thought, tear out my liver, devour my intestines. You won't ever kill me dead. Tomorrow when you come back I shall be here again. You will have to start anew on me. And every new day when the sun comes up. I shall never die. Not for you.

Khois, Khois, Khois.

My eyes were breaking. Earth, rock, trees, strange flowers, birds, animals, everything passed through my eyes. Journeys, panoramas, visions, mirages, desert, a subterranean river breaking through the surface. Years, ages, centuries, ancestors, descendants, bones, so many bones. The sheer whiteness of white.

Khois, Khois, Khois.

All I had ever had ran from my empty hands. All of it. Except this: somewhere in the land, I knew, somewhere, behind the thickets of euphorbia and burning aloes and undergrowth, was the child. He would live on. They could not kill me.

How dangerous it is to love.

And then I died, the first of my many deaths, as far as I can remember.

Glossary

(Unless otherwise indicated, these terms are all of Khoi origin.)

abba	to carry piggyback
abba skin	skin in which baby is strapped to mother's back
ati	reed pipes
baru	small milky bulb
bokmakierie (Afrikaans)	onomatopoeic bird name
buchu	fragrant herb with medicinal properties
chu'que	leader
dagga	indigenous hashish

dassie (Afrikaans)	rock rabbit
duiker (Afrikaans)	small antelope
gaib	magic medicine
Gaunab	the Evil One, who lives in the Black Sky
ghai skin	loincloth worn by men
gurah	string instrument
hadeda	a kind of ibis, regarded as a harbinger of death
hamerkop	hammerhead, a bird with visionary powers
"*Hebba ha*"	"Come back"
Heitsi-Eibib	great hunter ancestor, believed to have died and revived many times
igqira (Xhosa)	medicine man, witch doctor
kambro	wild bulb resembling a sweet potato
kanni	wild bulb
k'arakup	chameleon, a messenger from heaven
karba	earthenware vessel for storing liquids

Karoo	"Dry Place," the arid inland plains of the Cape
kaross	long garment made of skins sewn together
khoib	man
Khoikhoin	"people of people," designating the nomads known to colonists by the derogatory name of "Hottentots"
khois	woman
k'hrab	testicle
khuseti	the Pleiades
kierie	stick
kiewiet (Afrikaans)	onomatopoeic bird name
kloof (Afrikaans)	ravine
kombro	edible root
k'onkwa	Beard Men
koo bird	golden eagle
kraal	enclosure for sheep or cattle (corral)
kwekwa	(to have) sexual intercourse
lobola (Xhosa)	bride price
meerkat (Afrikaans)	ground squirrel
"Mutsi *atse*"	"I see you"
night walkers	evil spirits, succubi and incubi
njaba	wild bulb, resembling a truffle

piet-my-vrou (Afrikaans)	onomatopoeic bird name
riem (Afrikaans)	leather thong
San	nomadic hunter people, otherwise known by the derogatory name of "Bushmen"
sarês	an evil spirit in the form of a whirlwind
sibi	rain
Sobo khoin	People of the Shadows, spirits of the dead
Sonkwas	robbers, derogatory name for the San
tawete	gift offered as official greeting
t'gai aob	medicine man
t'gau	vagina
t'gauab	praying mantis, regarded as a sacred insect
thas jackal	an evil spirit in the form of a jackal
tinktinkie (Afrikaans)	a small wrenlike bird
T'*kaam*	Moon
T'*kama*	Big Bird, Ostrich
t'koi-t'koi	a kind of drum
t'nau	taboo, unclean
torob	war
tsamma	wild melon

Tsaob	The Smoldering Embers, the Milky Way
Tsui-Goab	God, the source of good, who lives in the Red Dawn
vlei (Afrikaans)	marsh

April–June 1985. January 1989. February 1990.